TRUST THE SAINT

*Six stories of the
incomparable Saint*

D1097192

LESLIE CHARTERIS

THE SAINT BOOKS

These are the titles in order of sequence
(the original titles are shown in brackets)

LESLIE CHARTERIS

TRUST THE SAINT

HODDER AND STOUGHTON

Copyright © 1962 by Leslie Charteris
First published October 1962
Hodder Paperback edition 1964
Second Impression 1966

Printed and bound in Great Britain for
Hodder and Stoughton Ltd.,
St. Paul's House, Warwick Lane,
London, E.C.4
by Hazell Watson & Viney Ltd.,
Aylesbury, Bucks

TO

AUDREY

for ten wonderful years

CONTENTS

THE HELPFUL PIRATE

THERE were a few people—a very few—within his tight circle of friends and almost astronomical orbit of acquaintances, for whom the Saint would do practically anything. Including even things which under any other auspices would have excited him to violent and voluble revolt.

One addiction that he especially despised was the fad for antiques. He could admire and love an old house for its own sake, but he was incapable of understanding anyone who would build a house today in good or bad imitation of the architecture of a bygone age. He could respect the furnishings of a genuine old house when they were its natural contemporaries, without necessarily wanting to live with them himself; but he could only wax sarcastic about dislocated decorators, professional or amateur, who put period furniture in a steel-and-glass skyscraper apartment.

"If the Georgians had been convinced that it wasn't smart to build anything but fake Elizabethan, there wouldn't have been any Georgian architecture for other monkeys to imitate. If Louis Seize had refused to park his ischial tuberosities on anything but an Henri Quatre chair, there wouldn't be any Louis Seize furniture for the fake factories to make copies of. In fact, if everyone had spent his time gazing adoringly backwards, we'd still be sleeping on stone cots in nice cosy caves. I was born in the twentieth century, and I don't see anything wrong with living with its better experiments."

He might have added that although he had been called

the twentieth century's brightest buccaneer, he had not found it necessary to leap around in thigh boots and ear-rings, with a cutlass between his teeth; but he still had some quite unpredictable modesties.

The bitterest focus of his prejudice, however, centred on the proliferation of the smaller shops that deal in the smaller items, the merchants of bric-a-brac rather than furniture, and their patrons.

"There's one on every other street in Europe, down to the smallest village," he had said. "If the non-edible con-tents of every trash can and junk pile for the last five centuries had been hidden away by gnomes, I doubt if the hoard would be enough to stock them all. There must be secret production lines that would make Detroit look like a medieval handicraft studio, running day and night to pour out enough antiques to meet the demand. And everywhere you can get to by jet plane or jalopy there's some beady-eyed tourist sniffing for a treasure that all his predecessors have overlooked. He wouldn't know a genuine William and Mary silver sugar-bowl from an early Woolworth, but so long as he's told it's more than two hundred years old he wants it. And if he's a she, which most of them are, she doesn't even want it for a sugar-bowl. She can see just how it could be re-modelled into the most darling lamp. And when she finds the most darling old lamp, she knows just how it could be eviscer-ated to make the cutest sugar-bowl. If Aladdin had run into one of them, the *Arabian Nights* would have been full of screaming genies."

Yet there he was, Simon Templar, in exactly that type of shop on the oddly named ABC-Strasse in Hamburg, Germany, saying to the proprietor:

"I was looking for some of those old Rhine wine glasses, the kind that spread out from under the bowl to the base, so that they stand on a sort of inverted ice-cream cone instead of a stem." He drew the shape in the air with both hands.

"Ah, yes, I know what you mean. They are called *Römer* glasses."

"Do you have any?"

"I am sorry, not at the moment. The old ones are quite rare."

"So I've heard. But I'm not worried about the price. Someone I want to do a special favour for is crazy about them, but he's only got two or three. I'd like to be able to give him a set. And the rarer and more valuable they are, the more he'll be impressed."

While the Saint, when it was necessary to play the part, could assume an aspect of proud or unprincipled poverty that would evoke a responsive twang from any normal heartstring, his usual appearance, fortunately or unfortunately, suggested a person who was so far on the other side of having been born with a silver spoon in his mouth that he must have been seriously shocked when he first learned that gold spoons were not standard issue. It was not merely the over-all excellence of his tailoring and accessories, for they were too superlative to be ostentatious. It was perhaps primarily an air, an attitude, the easy assurance of a man who has had the best for so long that he no longer demands it : he simply expects it.

The dealer was a broad-beamed portly burgher whose name, according to the legend on the shop window, was Johann Uhrmeister. He had receding sandy-grey hair and pale blue eyes which appraised the Saint as expertly as they would have rated any marketable relic.

"I should be glad to look around for you, sir. If you will leave your name——"

"Templar," Simon told him truthfully.

Germany was one country where he did not think he had earned much publicity, certainly not in recent years, and he did not expect his surname to elicit any reaction there, at least by itself. There was none from Uhrmeister as he wrote it down.

"And where are you staying?"

"At the *Vier Jahreszeiten*."

"If I can find any, I will let you know. How long are you staying here?"

"A week, maybe."

"It is your first time in Hamburg?"

"Yes."

Herr Uhrmeister turned and picked up a booklet from a stack on an inlaid table which was mainly burdened with a large and horrible gilt clock. The cover described it concisely as *An Introduction to Hamburg*. He gave it to Simon.

"Please take one of these, with our compliments. It may help you to enjoy your stay. And I hope you will be lucky in your search."

"Thank you," said the Saint.

He continued his quest through the remainder of the afternoon, on the same street and others, patiently ticking off the names of the shops on a list he had made from a classified directory before he started on the undertaking after lunch the previous day, and by closing time he could conscientiously claim to have tried them all. After having been half destroyed by the saturation bombings of 1943, the city had not only rebuilt itself but had succeeded in re-stocking its antique emporia almost as completely as its newest department stores. But in spite of the surprising roster of the former, the supply of "Roman" glasses (which is the literal translation of the name, though it would be harder still to find a prototype in Italy) had apparently lagged far behind that of other venerabilia, or else their rarity was not exaggerated. At the end of his pilgrimage he had seen two slightly chipped but probably authentic specimens, which did not match, and a line of crude souvenir reproductions emblazoned with corny coloured decals of local scenery, and had a more emphatic if not more respectful comprehension of those dedicated souls who did that sort of thing from their own enthusiasm and for their own pleasure.

It had been, he thought, an effort of extraordinary nobility, probably unprecedented and he devoutly hoped not soon to be called for again—a more profoundly heroic performance, for him, than taking on a half-dozen armed gorillas barehanded. But he was also a little footsore and extremely thirsty; and the alleviation of these conditions seemed more important for the moment than voting himself awards for altruism.

At the snug downstairs bar of the *Vier Jahreszeiten*— the Four Seasons Hotel, as the tourists prefer to render it —a long well-iced Peter Dawson and water soon began to assuage his most urgent aridity, an upholstered stool took the load off his metatarsals, and in a matter of minutes he had revived to the extent of being accessible to the standard civilized distractions.

"Not very nice weather, is it?" he remarked to the aloofly efficient bartender.

"No, sir," said the bartender pleasantly, but with the same aloof sufficiency, and left it at that.

It was evident that he either had been schooled against fraternizing with the customers or had no basic urge to do so beyond the fullest requirements of civility; and Simon felt no need to make a Herculean labour of changing that pattern of life. He pulled the *Introduction to Hamburg* from his pocket and began to read it.

It was much the same as any other guide-book of its type, except that it was free from any of the fractured English commonly found in such publications, which usually seem to have been prepared by some ambitious local school-teacher too jealous of his infallibility to submit to revision by a native-born Englishman or American. A note on the title-page said "Translated by Franz Kolben," but Mr. Kolben's style sounded more like Milwaukee than Heidelberg. Otherwise its thirty-two pages contained the usual descriptions of churches, museums, and monuments, listings of restaurants and cabarets, and a brief history of the town from the settlement established by Charlemagne in A.D. 811.

Simon Templar was not much of an *aficionado* of pure historical history, as you might call it; but here there was one paragraph which caught his eye as inevitably as a white nylon jig hooks a mackerel :

> Pirates controlled the Elbe until 1402, when Klaus Störtebeker, the greatest of them, was captured and beheaded on the Grasbrook. What happened to the treasure he extorted in gold and silver and jewels is still a mystery. He is said to have hidden a map of its whereabouts in the base of a pewter goblet on which he carved his initials suspended from a gallows, but it has never been found.

The Saint sighed invisibly.

Perhaps it was an encouraging symptom of inexhaustible youth that he could still feel a quickening of the pulse at such a romantic image. Yet there was a sombre index of maturity in the fact that he was content to pigeonhole it as an amusing legend, instead of being inspired to set out on the trail of the clue.

Nevertheless, Franz Kolben, who had created the myth

entirely out of his own head, would have felt highly complimented by the tribute to his invention.

Simon read through to the end of the brochure without finding anything else of comparable interest. In the meantime a young woman had come in and sat down at the other end of the short counter. He had glanced up automatically, and noted with pleasure that she was blonde and shapely of both face and figure : it would have been easier to label her "a girl", but she had the confidence of the mid-twenties and her outfitting had been assembled with well-seasoned sophistication. He was too old a hand to stare any longer, but had heard her order a champagne cocktail in English that had an American intonation but still seemed to have a slight Germanic accent. He had philosophically refrained from speculating any further. No doubt she would soon be joined and abducted by some upper-echelon American salesman on the European circuit, or some equally crass Rhineland industrialist—or something similarly cut, dried, and pre-emptive. He was a long time past building day-dreams on her obvious foundations.

But now, as he put the pamphlet back in his pocket and gave her another studiously casual glance, he found her looking directly at him with a candour which disclaimed all such prior commitments.

"Would you help me?" she said.

He smiled with just the right degree of diffidence—not eagerly enough to look like a bumpkin, but not so distantly as to be discouraging.

"Tell me how."

"Are you on your own here? I mean, do you have a wife with you, or anything?"

"Not even anything."

"I only ask," she explained, "because I don't want to give you a problem because of mine."

He was a trifle puzzled.

"You mean you have a husband—or something?"

"Oh, no. If I had, I wouldn't have to do this. I have a problem because I want someone to go out with for the evening, and I don't know anyone here. I don't want you to take me out and pay for everything, because that would give you the wrong idea. But I can't offer to pay, because that would insult you. Would it be all right if we went Dutch?"

If that was the local line, it at least had an element of novelty. Now that it was permissible to scrutinize her more thoroughly, however, he was able to observe that her dress was smartly but soberly tailored, and she wore none of the usual colouration of a professional lady of the evening. Perhaps that also was a local custom—but what could he lose by going along with it a little farther?

"Let me buy a drink, anyhow," he said, "and we could sit down and talk it over."

Until then they had been the only two customers, but now a trio of Italian salesmen had come in and were piling on to the intervening bar stools, noisily debating their designs upon the Common Market. The Saint's new acquaintance moved quietly to a table in a corner, where he joined her. The disinterested bartender brought the drinks, and Simon listened to her.

"I know this must all sound a little crazy, but I'm a tourist too, and I've heard that there's a street here which is much wilder than Montmartre, and I wanted to see it, but I can't go there alone."

"Hardly, from what I've been reading," he agreed. "And you want someone to chaperone you on a sight-seeing tour of the dens of iniquity."

"Could you stand it? I'm curious, that's all, and a woman is so handicapped in some ways, if she is a little respectable."

"I shall treasure the implied compliment," he murmured. "And I'd be delighted to see the sights with you. I must admit that I'm curious too, even if I'm not as respectable as I look."

With his rakehell profile and impudent blue eyes, this was a statement of highly questionable validity, but she refrained from taking issue with it. Although her pink and white and flaxen allure was happily not built upon operatic proportions, she seemed to have a certain Wagnerian solemnity which was a piquant contrast to what she was proposing.

"And you are free tonight?" she asked. "Or would you prefer another time?"

"Tonight. If we put it off, you might lose your curiosity —or your nerve." His gaze continued to analyze her shrewdly but not antagonistically. "But if you won't mind my asking, what kind of tourist are you? You speak English perfectly, but you still have just a little accent, and a way of putting things——"

"Of course. I'm half German. I was born in Munich. My mother was an American, but when the last war came she stayed here with my father. But she would talk only English to me, so I never forgot it. Sometimes when I come in a place like this I forget which language I should be talking."

"But you said you were a tourist here."

"You make me feel so foolish—like someone from Chicago who must admit she's in New York for the first time. But in Europe everyone hasn't always been everywhere."

"Nor has everyone in America," said the Saint consolingly. "In fact, there are several people in New York who've never been to Brooklyn."

"I'd like to go to New York. And Brooklyn, too. I think I'd feel much more at home there than in Hamburg, with all I've heard about them and seen in American movies."

"Do you still live in Munich?"

"Yes. I work there, for a shipping company. So I'm answering letters from America all the time." It seemed to remind her of a formality that had so far been omitted from their informal acquaintance. "My name is Eva."

He wondered whether this limited identification was another accepted local discretion or her own idea. But by falling in step without questioning it, he could conveniently by-pass his own perennial problem.

"Mine is Simon."

She was a pleasant companion in spite of her incongruous seriousness, and the Saint was especially contented to have acquired her at that hour, for he hated to eat alone. His friend had recommended the new penthouse restaurant atop the Bavaria Brewery, overlooking the port, and presently they took a taxi there to lay a foundation for the night's work.

"We must have eel soup," she said as they considered the menus. "It's one of the things Hamburg is famous for. Unless the idea shocks you?"

"What else goes into it—besides eels?"

"Vegetables, and herbs, and a sort of little dumpling, and prunes."

"It sounds frightful," he said. "But I'll make the experiment, if you want to."

Actually it turned out to be completely delectable, in an off-beat sweet-sour way. Afterwards they had the *Vierländer Mastgeflügel*, a tender broiled chicken, and a bottle of Deinhard's Hanns Christof Wein of '59—that greatest year of the decade for the vineyards of the Rhine. And under the combination of mellowing influences their acquaintance warmed and ripened. She didn't become unexpectedly stimulating and exciting, but she was absorbently easy to be with.

They sat beside one of the long plate-glass windows commanding a panorama of docks and warehouses and their associated machinery to which night and artificial lights lent an obviously meretricious but seductive glamour; and once when an attentive head-waiter came by, Eva gestured outwards and asked: "What is that?"

"It is all part of the harbour of Hamburg. Just over there it is called the *Grasbrook Hafen*."

Simon sat up.

"Not the place where good old Klaus Störtebeker got it in the neck—if I may use the expression?"

"Yes, that is the same place. But it would have looked much different then."

"What are you talking about?" Eva asked, as the head-waiter moved on.

"An old-time pirate in these parts," said the Saint. "I was reading about him in a guide-book just before we met. He left a buried treasure somewhere, too."

"How romantic!" Her cornflower-blue eyes danced with more animation than they had previously revealed. "Tell me about it."

He brought out the little book and read her the passage which had captivated him.

"But I'm afraid," he concluded, "that if you want to get rich quick you'll have to think of something faster than looking for a goblet with a gallows on it."

"I suppose so." She was almost as crestfallen as if the goblet had been on the table and a *commis* had whisked it away with the soup plates. "There are no adventures of that kind any more."

Of all men alive, few could have produced better grounds to contest that assertion; but for the moment Simon Templar preferred not to cite them. Instead, he said: "We'll have to do the best we can with our own adventure. Is there anything special you want to see on the Reeperbahn?"

"Everything."

"That might be a rather wide order."

"I've heard they have women who wrestle in a tank full of mud."

"Well, that might be a fairly romantic start," he admitted. "I guess we could try that for an *hors d'oeuvre*, and play it by ear from there."

The Reeperbahn in Hamburg (which once meant "The Street of Rope Workers") has long since lost its nautical connotation, except as regards the transient sailors who have made it the essential symbol of their port of call. It has become to Hamburg what Montmartre became to the tourist in Paris—who has no relationship with the Parisian. Along its few short blocks and up some of the side streets which lead off it is clustered a variety of establishments catering to the most generally deplored forms of human indulgence which even the citizens of Sodom and Gomorrah might have contemplated with some respect. But unlike those classic citadels of depravity, the Reeperbahn, which was also destroyed by fire from the heavens delivered by the air raiders of World War II, has risen again from the ashes with still more reprehensible vigour and the added modern advantages of coruscating neon.

There is available every gratification traditionally craved by the male animal on a toot, from the brassy ballroom to the dim-lighted cabaret, from the costumed chorus to the table-top strip-tease, from the extrovert's parade of flesh to the introvert's pornography, literate or pictorial, still or motion picture, with companionship from overdressed to undressed, with all the necessary alcohols to make everything enticing, if you take enough of them —or, if you are harder to intoxicate, and want to seek just a little harder, more costly but more powerful narcotics. It is all there, with the effort of search scaled down to the minimum which any aspiring debauchee should be able to muster, or he should give up and stay home. Everything from the oldest sensations to the newest variations—down to such exotic eccentricities as the principal attraction at the *Jungmühle*, where they had agreed to start their sampling.

Simon and Eva sat at a front table in an auditorium like a small converted theatre, in which the side walls near the stage were smeared and stained with peculiar splash marks which suggested that past performers had pelted an unappreciative audience with unsavoury tokens of their indignation, instead of being thus showered themselves by dissatisfied spectators according to the antique custom. The reality and actuality of this wild hypothesis was promptly concretized by a servitor who arrived with two large sheets of plastic and politely but matter-of-factly indicated that they should be tucked on like over-sized bibs before even ordering anything spillable.

"I shall drink beer all the time," Eva said rather primly. "It's the cheapest thing to order, and it's always safe even in the worst places, and we shouldn't get drunk in the first dive or two we try."

"I suppose that's a sound approach," said the Saint, with respect.

The superannuated discard of a travelling opera company who had been sentimentally vocalizing on the stage bowed off, with the muted approval of the congregation; a tarpaulin cover was removed from what might have been a shallow orchestra pit, revealing that it had been converted into a kind of wading trough paved with moist brown muck; the spotlights brightened, and two women entered from opposite wings and met in the centre of the stage, draped in vivid satin robes which they threw off as the loudspeakers identified them. Underneath they wore only bikini trunks and their own exuberant flesh and glands. The formalities having been complied with, they seized each other by the hair and fell into the tank with a juicy splash.

Thereafter it was much the same as the traditional ballet popularized in the commercial guise of wrestling by hundreds of artistes of the grunt and grimace and groan, except that these performers not only had an opportunity to illustrate the more delicate and sensitive feminine approach but had a shallow quagmire of lusciously textured sludge to do it in. This gave them a few extra vulnerable targets to kick, twist, and gouge, and an additional weapon to bring into play. While one of them was attempting to suffocate the other by grinding her face into the mud, she could suffer the indignity of having her panties pulled down and stuffed with the same goo; and when not so intertwined they could throw gobs of it in each other's faces, which if inaccurately aimed might splatter the scenery or the onlookers—which explained the spray flecks on the walls and the considerately furnished bibs. By the time this tender choreography had run its course, both the exponents were decently covered from crown to toe with a succulent coating of gunk, and their sex appeal was almost equal to that of two hippopotami emerging from a wallow.

Simon, dividing his clinical attention between the grappling amazons and Eva, was somewhat nonplussed by her reaction, or the lack of it. She seemed to be neither startled, nor shocked, nor disgusted, nor embarrassed, nor morbidly fascinated, by these revelations of the infinite range of female grace and tenderness. The most you could have said, based on her outward placidity, was that she was mildly amused. It was none of the obvious responses that he would have expected of a woman so bent on experience that she had to pick up a stranger in a bar to facilitate it.

"Shall we sit out another minuet?" he inquired. "Or should we move on?"

"I think we should try something else," she replied with the same demure detachment. "Do you know—you won't believe me—I've never seen a strip-tease?"

"I believe that can be easily remedied," he said, with the same gravity.

The German strip-tease follows much the same pattern as the American original, but with characteristic efficiency it moves much more briskly towards the essential objective, which is that the teaser should strip. In the opinion of many students, this leads to what might be paradoxically called a decent haste in the peeling. The esoteric stimuli of the bump and grind have never enslaved many addicts in Europe; but to replace that allure the German ecdysiast has the advantage of a law which permits her to expose every last square centimetre of her person provided she does not wiggle it. Therefore with studious legality even the G-string is twanged off during a momentary blackout before the final climax, or not even bothered with in incidental tableaux, and the uncomplicated connoisseur of nudity can be assured of 100 per cent satisfaction.

On and around the Reeperbahn, the problem is not to find a place that features this kind of entertainment but to decide which one to patronize. Each of them has its panegyrist outside to buttonhole the passer-by and extol the lewd delights within. The first such temple of voyeurism that Simon picked at random, however, failed so drably to live up to its eulogy that he could not quite make himself accept it as a single and final sample of what the town could offer in that line, and he himself suggested one more try. Their next gamble was the *Colibri*; and there the density of the crowd which happily shared its tables on a basis of vacant chairs rather than acquaintance indicated that it relied less on a barker outside than on a clientele that knew its way around. The supposition was rapidly justified : the exhibitionists averaged younger and comelier, and disrobed with a continuing celerity that would have given even a jaded sultan no cause for complaint.

But Eva watched this with no perceptible difference from the way she had viewed the lamentable display in the preceding joint—without horror or excitement, but with a sort of tepid amusement that narrowly escaped the suspicion of boredom.

"Is it what you expected?" he asked, when she caught his eyes on her instead of on the latest playful grouping of naked maidens.

"More or less."

"You don't seem to get much of a kick out of it."

"Did you expect me to? A normal woman shouldn't get much of a kick out of watching other women undress, should she?"

"I was wondering why you were so keen to do it."

"To know just what people mean when they talk about these shows, and what it is that they go to see. You see,

I'm really terribly innocent, and yet a woman hates to be called unsophisticated. But I can admit it to you, because you don't know any of my friends, and after this I shall know as much as they do."

He was certainly not qualified to confirm or contest that, but it was a divertingly novel approach. He said: "Now what would you like to add to your education?"

"I've heard there's a street of little houses, where the girls sit in the windows or make bargains at the doors."

There was such a street, or alley, and they obtained directions to it without difficulty; but at the half-barricaded entrance they were barred by a stodgily correct *Polizist*.

"Very sorry," he said in English, recognizing automatically that only foreigners attempted this transgression. "Not for ladies. Men only."

"How silly," she pouted as they walked away after a brief futile argument. "There are women in there already, aren't there?"

"But only on business," Simon pointed out. "I can understand how they could resent being stared at like specimens in a zoo, by other women who'd never done that kind of work. But perhaps you didn't know that it can be work."

She gave him a sharp defensive glance, which he blandly pretended not to notice. He seemed to be merely looking around for some other potential source of the sophistication she wanted.

"There must be some way for a man to meet a girl that is not so cold-blooded," she said at last. "You must have had some experience in that way. I can't see you going in that closed street to buy a woman. But what else would you do?"

He forbore from mentioning that he had not done so

badly by just sitting at the bar of a first-class hotel. They
were at the corner of another turning, down which the
darkness was splintered by a blazing frontage of all-
purpose brilliance topped by a vertical arrangement of
fluorescent tubes which spelled the name *Silbersack*.

"If I were a sailor on the loose," he said, remembering
bygone days in far-off ports when he had been little more
than that, "I'd probably try my luck in a joint something
like that."

The inside was as stark and garish as the outside. There
was no attempt at *décor*, merely a practical provision of
seats and tables. Girls and women in street clothes that
made no pretension of glamour, and ordinary-looking
men of mostly middle and lower ages in even more un-
distinguished tailorings, stood around or sat and drank
and/or eyed each other and/or danced in a minimum of
empty floor space to the rhythms of a juke box.

Simon and Eva sat on a bench in a corner and ordered
more beer. A peripatetic artist of curiously ageless aspect
came by, whipped out a pair of nail scissors, and snipped
away at a piece of plain paper which, unfolded, separated, and swiftly pasted to two plain white cards, became
a mirror-pair of their two silhouettes in black cut-out.
The likenesses were extraordinary. Simon registered his
appreciation with largesse which was apparently exces-
sive, for the artist beamingly began snipping again. The
scissors twinkled and flew; and out of their quicksilver
nibbling came another mirror-pair of silhouettes, only this
time it was a pastoral whimsy, a boy and a girl and a
fawn framed in a woodland bower, all filigreed in a
couple of minutes with a delicacy and truth of line that
many a competent draughtsman would have been glad to
achieve with a pen in half an hour. The snipper presented
those shadowgraphs as a reciprocal bonus, with a smile

and a bow, and went away; but for Simon Templar, who had his own peculiarly slanted scale of values, this was the happiest highlight of the evening so far.

"I think this is rather dull," Eva said.

The Saint by that time was beginning to feel unwontedly adaptable.

"What would you suggest next?" he asked.

"There are special movies, aren't there, which are only shown privately?"

"There are such things. But I don't think you'd like them."

"Then we can walk out. But I'd like to know *why* I didn't like them."

"They mightn't be so easy to find. Even around here, they're probably illegal."

"At least we can inquire."

"And expensive."

She opened her eyes wider.

"But we agreed to go Dutch. Are you running short? Or do you think I wasn't serious?" She opened her bag and took out a small wad of currency held in a clip, from which she pulled three hundred-mark notes. "Here—when we settle up, you give me the change, if there is any."

Simon put away the deposit unblushingly, with the impersonal courtesy of a banker. They went out again, and he said : "I suppose one of those touts on the Reeperbahn could tell us what the chances are."

"Let's go this way." She pointed. "It looks a nice sinister street."

He thought that its sinister air was probably only an illusion compounded of grime and bad lighting, but he automatically set himself on the alert for any flicker of a shadow or whisper of sound that would give split-second warning of a sneak attack. It seemed rather far-fetched to imagine that she would have gone through such a long and roundabout routine merely to set him up for a rendezvous with a mugger; but he had survived far beyond any reasonable expectation for a man of his proclivities largely because he never completely ruled out any such possibilities, however remote. But at the same time taking the likelier line that there was no such sordid anticlimax in store, he was trying to decide at what point he should set a limit to the depths of depravity to which a gentleman could properly escort a scientifically inquisitive lady, whilst toying with his own scientific temptation to find out how far she would go before calling off the experiment.

And then all these avenues of speculation dead-ended suddenly and electrifyingly as they came down to within a few yards of the Reeperbahn again, without any incident, and yet Eva abruptly stopped in her tracks and clutched the Saint's arm as if she had been confronted by a rampaging ogre.

It was nothing so spectacular that she pointed at, however. Nothing but the window of a side-street pawnshop, located there to accommodate patrons of the main drag who might find themselves temporarily embarrassed for the wherewithal to prolong a promising spree. Inside the window were spread and stacked and suspended the weird miscellaneous pledges of uncounted revellers who had moved on and left their collateral unredeemed, every conceivable form of security from cufflinks to clarinets.

And near the centre of the window was a tarnished pewter goblet.

On which were crudely carved the initials "KS".

Suspended, Simon saw, as Eva dragged him closer, from the scratched outline of a gibbet . . .

"That's *it*, isn't it?" she breathed. "The goblet that it tells about in your guide-book!"

"It couldn't be," he said mechanically.

"But it *is*! It's exactly like the book describes it—the initials, the gallows, *everything*!"

The Saint stared at it. He couldn't go on arguing with what she said. And yet he was in the same state of incredulous shock that must stun anyone who sees the number of his ticket listed as the winner of some National Lottery or the Irish Sweep. It was the thing that everybody has daydreamed of but recognized realistically that it will never happen. And yet, even more inescapably than a bolt of lightning, it has to strike someone, somewhere.

But in this instance, the chronicler must now reveal, the lightning was no electrical phenomenon. It was the stroke of genius of Franz Kolben, perhaps the most financially successful though inglorious author that Hamburg has ever known.

A little belated background may here be necessary.

Mr. Franz Kolben (who formerly preferred to be known as "Frank") was, as the Saint had somewhat intuitively divined, in fact a born native of Milwaukee, U.S.A., an off-sprout of German immigrants who had raised him bilingually with better motives than he had ever applied to this advantage. Leaving home as soon as he could dispense with its fringe benefits, young Frank had found employment in a modern furniture factory in Grand Rapids, from which he graduated to a more exclusive atelier in Chicago which fabricated equally modern antiques. From there, since he was an ambitious and go-ahead type with wits as sharp as any chisel, it was another logical step from the manufacturing to the retailing side, which not only paid better but offered more scope to his developing ingenuity, and enlarged his vision

from the limited area of phony period furniture to the
entire field of bogus antiquity. He was in a fair way to
becoming the beardless wonder of the racket in that region
when the draft finally netted him and unfeelingly trans-
muted him from an operator to a number in an operation.

World War II had reached its supposedly glorious conclusion about the time Sergeant Kolben had finally convinced the arbiters of his destiny that his knowledge of
German entitled him to an occupation billet in Europe
rather than a combat assignment in the Pacific. To his
indescribable chagrin, he had presented his case so convincingly that no subsequent effort could change his
orders, and in due inexorable course he found himself in
Hamburg, a very small cog in the Military Government,
replacing some lucky veteran with enough points to be
heading for home and honourable discharge.

With all his faults, however, Franz Kolben had never
been a quitter, and he wasted less time than many more
honest men in unprofitable pining. His background and
knowledge inevitably trended him in one particular direction; and when he detected one of the earliest traders to
come out of hiding in the act of selling a battle-happy GI
a piece of cheap china guaranteed to be genuine old
Dresden lovingly cached through *blitz* and *krieg*, he knew
he had it made. What might have begun and ended in
less talented hands as a rudimentary exercise in blackmail,
blossomed under Frankie's green-hungry thumbs into an
industry which may have mulcted the warriors homing
from its range of more hard-earned dollars than any temptation but sex. To this day, there are probably few com-
munities in America where you could not find some
spurious souvenir of German liberation which Kolben had
helped to produce.

But there came a time at last when all the well-heeled

buyers had been repatriated, and even Master Sergeant Kolben was eligible for discharge; and Frankie found to his astonishment that he was not yet ready to go home. He had done all right and he had evolved notions of doing better, and he had also formed a sentimental attachment which satisfied all his desires in that zone. He decided to stay on; and his hunch was right. Very soon the free-spending soldiery was replaced by prosperous German industrialists from the Rhineland and the South, and then they in turn were diluted by the first venturesome trickle of civilian tourists from former enemy countries, a trickle which swelled rapidly into a tide, which washed up a regular supply of suckers on the doorstep of Frankie's very satisfied partner—whose name, we need no longer conceal, was Uhrmeister.

The *Introduction to Hamburg* had been one of Frankie's sublimest inspirations, and he had worked hard on it, despite the fact that he had cribbed practically all its information from other publications. The labour of assembling, rearranging, and paraphrasing the material sufficiently to evade suit for infringements of copyright had been surprisingly arduous, for he had no natural literary inclination, but it was fully rewarded by the opportunity to inject the one sentence which was completely and incontrovertibly original with him :

He is said to have hidden a map of its whereabouts in the base of a pewter goblet on which he carved his initials suspended from a gallows, but it has never been found.

"Where did you read this, Franz?" asked Uhrmeister when he saw the manuscript—he could never get used to addressing his associate, who spoke German as well as he did himself, by anything but the German name. "I lived here all my life, and this is the first time I heard it."

"I made it up, Papa," Frankie admitted cheerfully. "But it is the most important thing in the book. Remember, to almost any tourist, a guide-book is like gospel. He may not believe what *you* tell him—but everything he reads in a book, he believes. So when you see a likely mark, you don't tell him anything. You give him the book."

Herr Uhrmeister, who was no *dummkopf*, but who had questioned why he should invest in the printing of a guide-book superficially like any other guide-book, but to be dispensed gratuitously in certain locations without even mentioning the name of his shop, began to catch on.

"Now, we must begin to make these goblets."

For some time they had sold very well indeed, if not like hot cakes, perhaps more appropriately like gold bricks, as they appeared in other places not ostensibly connected with Herr Uhrmeister's establishment on ABC-Strasse, at preposterously inflated prices which were seldom questioned by buyers in a panic to get away with their purchase before anyone else saw it and outbid them, or the vendor realized what he was parting with.

The fact that the bases of the goblets, when cut into or broken open, proved to contain nothing but dust and air, did not constitute fraud under any statute; and in any case the hardihood of a buyer who would have brought formal complaint about having been cheated out of what he hoped to cheat the seller was practically inconceivable. Probably there was not one in a hundred who even suspected that he had been more than just unlucky. Nevertheless, after a while Frank Kolben's restless mind perceived where the wheeze was falling short of its maximum potential pay-off, and went back to work to remedy that——

"If that's Klaus Störtebeker's own original goblet," Simon persisted, "why is it still there? Why hasn't someone else seen it and bought it before this? If it comes to that, why is the pawnbroker selling it?"

"Perhaps he hasn't heard the story," Eva responded. "Why should a little pawnbroker know everything? Why should everyone who passes know it? If we had passed last night instead of tonight, before you read that book, would we have known? At least I am not going to laugh at it and go away!"

She released his arm with a movement that was almost like throwing away something that had become distasteful, and turned to the door of the shop. It opened for her with a loud jangling of bells; the lights had always been on inside, and through the window Simon could see the presumable proprietor shuffle out through the curtains behind the counter at the back—an old man whose trade had plainly left him no illusions and even less patience with anybody who expected him to harbour one. The shop was apparently still open, ready to finance anyone who came by with acceptable security.

By the time Simon caught up with Eva inside, she already had the proprietor at a disadvantage in the less familiar aspect of buyer-seller relations, for such places.

"Are you crazy?" she was saying in German. "Three hundred marks—for a battered old thing like that?"

"It is very old," said the shopkeeper, like a recitation. "Perhaps of the fifteenth century."

"Then it is so much more secondhand. I will pay two hundred."

"That is absurd, gracious lady. Perhaps two hundred and ninety——"

Simon picked up the goblet and examined it more closely. Judging by its weight, the stem and base seemed to be hollow, but they were solidly plugged at the bottom. He studied the construction and the sealing while the haggling ran its predestined course.

"Two hundred and forty, then. Not a *pfennig* more!"

"Very well." The final despondent shrug. "But only because you are too beautiful, and I am too old and tired——"

Since the pawnbroker was an indigent, mildly alcoholic, pensioned-off uncle of Johann Uhrmeister, he knew when to cut the bargaining and clinch the sale.

Eva counted the money out of her own purse, quickly but precisely, and almost snatched the goblet out of Simon's hands as she headed out of the shop.

He stayed with her patiently for a few yards along the Reeperbahn again, where she led him into a dazzlingly dreadful all-night restaurant. He followed her into a corner booth, where she ordered ham sandwiches and beer for both of them and put the goblet on the marble tabletop and leered at it as if it had been a prize they had won in a fun fair.

"Let's get it open," she said.

"I'll need some sort of tool for that," he told her. "The base is filled with some sort of solder. I can't dig it out with a fork."

"You could break the stem off, couldn't you?"

He raised his eyebrows.

"After you just paid sixty dollars for it?"

"It was not bought to keep on a mantelpiece. I am too excited to wait. Break it!"

"Okay, if you say so."

He picked up the goblet endways in two hands, and bent and twisted. It came apart at the junction of cup and stem, without too much resistance from the soft metal. And within the hollow stem they saw the end of a scroll—which *could* be dug out with a fork.

It was a piece of parchment rolled to about the size of a panatela, and stained with what most people would have taken for age but Franz Kolben could have told them was cold tea. Simon loosened and spread it with reverent care. The ink on it had also aged, to the colour of dark rust, with the help of another of Mr. Kolben's chemical tricks of the trade. The lettering at the top had involved more laborious research, but in convincingly medieval Gothic characters it announced :

$\mathfrak{Hier\ heff\ it\ mienen\ Schat\ inpurrt}$

Simon spelled it out with frowning difficulty which ended in irritated puzzlement.

"I thought I could get by in German," he complained, "but what the hell does that mean?"

"It's old German, of course," she said, leaning close to his shoulder. "This was written more than five hundred years ago! In modern German it would be *'Dies ist der Platz wo ich meinen Schatz vergrub'*—'This is where I buried my treasure'."

"Can you read the rest?"

There was a crude map, or combination of map and drawing, as was the ancient custom. It showed a river at the bottom with ships on it, a recognizable church, and a narrow two-storey house, intricately half-timbered, and a distinctive high-peaked roof with gables surmounted by a conical-topped turret. So much the Saint saw, and was trying unsuccessfully to decipher the cramped and spiky script which filled the other half of the sheet when Eva snatched it out of his fingers and put it in her purse.

"I will read it later," she said.

He showed his astonishment.

"Aren't you too excited to wait any more?"

"Yes. But you've seen enough already—perhaps too much."

"Are you afraid I might rush off and beat you to this treasure and take off with your share?"

"My share," she said, "is all of it. Why should you have any? For breaking open the goblet? I bought it!"

"I thought this evening was supposed to be fifty-fifty," he said slowly.

She shifted farther away from him, defensively.

"That was only for the food and drink and the shows, nothing else. The goblet was my own. Let anyone ask the man in the shop who paid for it."

"You didn't need to do that. I thought you only did it because you'd done all the talking."

"I didn't ask you to buy it. I decided for myself. And who saw it first. I did. You would have walked past and never seen it if I had not stopped you. And even then you said it couldn't be the one. It was I who went in the shop!"

To record that this was one of the rare occasions when Simon Templar was totally flabbergasted would be an understatement of laconic grandeur. But there was no doubt that she meant it all.

He tried one more appeal to higher ethics : "And why would you have been interested if I hadn't shown you that bit in my guide-book?"

"All the thousands of people who must have read it could say that," she scoffed. "And then the man who wrote the book would say that *he* had the best claim."

Franz Kolben would have been proud of her.

The Saint might also have merited official sanctification if he had not had to subdue an unhallowed masculine impulse to remodel her pretty but obnoxiously self-satisfied face with one eloquent set of knuckles, but he was catatonically immobilized by an insuperable reluctance to sink to the level of some of his latter-day imitators. But he still had a tattered sense of humour.

"All right," he said. "Here's your change." He made a rough calculation, counted out money, and pushed it towards her. "Have fun—and don't buy any more mugs."

She took the change without demur, like a God-given right, and put it away where she had put the parchment. She had no sense of humour that vibrated with his.

"Now let me out," she said, and the clutch on her handbag was no tighter than the set of her mouth. "If you try to stop me, or follow me, I call the police."

The Saint could usually rise to an occasion, but this was one that had been immutably taken out of his hands. He was caught at a disadvantage that would have baffled anyone. If she had been a man, there might have been a remedy, even if it involved physical violence; but to start anything so drastic with her, in such a crowded place or the equally bright and busy street outside, would have only been inviting certain arrest on the most ignominious charges.

He moved aside, and she picked up the two broken pieces of the goblet and stepped past him.

"Thank you," she said stiffly, "for taking me out."

"Thank *you*," he murmured, with a subtlety that surely went over her head, "for taking *me*."

He watched her exit, reflecting wryly that it was sometimes hard to maintain the attitude of a knight-errant towards womankind in the light of such revelations of what cupidity could do to their rectitude.

He paid the bill and went out, but by the time he reached the street she was nowhere to be seen. This was nothing like any conclusion that he had anticipated from their brief encounter, but he was philosopher enough to find some compensation in the discovery that after all life still had some surprises left. And the night had not been completely wasted, for in the course of their peregrinations he had found one other thing which he had come to Hamburg to look for.

He walked back to the *Silbersack*, and ordered a beer, and caught the eye of the roving silhouette-cutter. The man came over, beaming, with scissors already twinkling. Simon let him proceed, but took from his pocket another silhouette—not one of those he had recently seen cut, but identical in style and mounting. He showed it.

"Is this one of yours?"

"Yes, that is my work."

"Do you remember the man?"

The artist's friendliness seemed to begin to dwindle fractionally.

"That is difficult. *Man sieht so viele Leute.* Is he a friend of yours?"

"He sent this picture to a friend of mine, and I wondered where he had it made. Was he here with anyone that you know?"

The other's face became finally blank.

"*Man kann sich nicht an jeden erinnern.* I am sorry, I have quite forgotten."

Simon laid a hundred-mark note on the table.

"Couldn't you remember if you tried?"

The silhouettist swiftly separated the black profiles he had cut, pasted them on cards, and pushed back the money.

"*Danke schön,*" he said, "you already paid me too much. I am sorry that I can do no more for you, but neither do I want to make trouble for anyone. In this quarter I have learned to mind my own business."

His smile flashed again as he moved away.

Simon decided that he had had all he wanted for one night, and went home.

At breakfast the next morning he opened his guide-book again, turning this time to the section on "Old Hamburg". The day was chilly and drizzly, more inducive to armchair exploration than to outdoor sightseeing, but he finally put on a trench coat and drove himself out nevertheless to take the recommended ramble. Following the suggested route with the aid of a map, he walked by way of the Rathausmarkt to the St Katharinen chapel, and thence to inspect the old mansions on the Deich-strasse overlooking the Nikolaifleet canal. Picturesque as they were, none of them came within range of matching the sketch he had seen on the parchment.

After a decent break for lunch, he went on up by the St Nikolai across to the Kleine Michaeliskirche and on to the great St Michaelis church, "Der Michael" as it is called by the citizens, which is still one of the landmarks of the town. But most of the other original buildings in that area had been razed by the bombings, and where there were not still empty spaces there were mostly modernistic shops and apartments. At the end of another long block to the west he found another church in the Zeughausmarkt, but it was a very obviously post-war restoration. Then he started back along Hütten, and had a hesitant resurgence of hope as he came to a few old timber-frame houses there, and more on the Peterstrasse which branched off it. But nothing corresponded even remotely with what he had seen on the map that came from the goblet, though he zigzagged and crisscrossed through every side street and alley in the precinct.

Of course, it would have been fairly fantastic if the result had been any different. Without benefit of the hieroglyphics which he had been unable to read, he might have tramped aimlessly around the city for days without finding a church and a house something like a primitive drawing which he had only seen for a few seconds. In fact, the instructions might have eliminated Hamburg altogether. They might have referred to any village in North Germany, anywhere along the Elbe. He had simply treated himself to some fairly fresh air and moderate exercise, while time went by that might have been spent more usefully. After all, he had come there to look for a man, not to be wild-goosed into a fanciful treasure hunt.

He had concentrated on only two clues : that the man was harmlessly nutty on antiques, and that the last communication from him had been a cut-out silhouette pasted on a blank card and mailed back to his daughter with scrawled greetings and the bare announcement that he was enjoying himself. Simon Templar had merely tried to weave a similar course in the hope that he might trip over a trail.

"I never promised to go straight after the War," he had protested to the man who telephoned him from Washington, who was known only as Hamilton. "And anyhow I'm enjoying my retirement. Why don't you nurse your own babies?"

"Just this once," Hamilton wheedled. "This chap is very important. As a matter of fact, we haven't even let out a word that he's missing. If he's actually gone over to the Other Side, it's not going to be funny. We can't write him off till we know there's no chance of getting him back."

And that was as stale a bait as any game fish ever rose to, Simon retrospected as he achieved his weary return at cocktail time to the embalming basement of the *Vier Jahreszeiten.*

And there, already sitting at the corner table which they had occupied some twenty-four hours earlier, was Eva.

She looked up and saw him, and smiled with a tremulous invitation which was a disintegrative switch from the atmosphere in which they had parted. But the Saint was not petty enough to turn that into a barrier.

He veered towards her as if they had had a date all the time, and he had only just seen her, and said: "Are we going Dutch again, or are you buying?"

"Please have a drink," she said.

He ordered a double Peter Dawson, and left her to continue.

"I hoped you would come back here," she said. "I was so ashamed of myself after last night. It's terrible what money will do to your thinking. Can you ever forgive me?"

"That depends," he said calmly. "How much am I offered?"

"I found the house," she said. "With the directions, it wasn't so hard."

He sat down.

"Where?"

"In St Pauli. I asked questions, and found out it was the oldest part of Hamburg. So I looked there, and I found it. But it was not for sale."

"Very likely."

"But I rang the doorbell. The man was most unpleasant. He said he was happy there, and he didn't want to sell his house to anyone. Then I had a wonderful idea. I said I was from a movie company, and we would like to rent it for a little while, just for a few shots——Then he began to be a little interested."

Simon's drink came, and he raised the glass to her and sipped.

"And you made a deal?"

"Well, yes and no. He talked a lot about what a nuisance it would be for him to move out, and the personal things he'd have to pack up, and the damage that might be done, and his invalid mother who would be so upset at being moved, and why should he have so much inconvenience when he was not hard up for a few marks. But at last he said that we could rent it for two weeks for fifty thousand marks."

Simon's lips shaped a whistle.

"Twelve thousand five hundred dollars—that's probably half what the house is worth."

"At least a quarter. But he said it would be as much trouble for him as if he was renting it for two years, and he would not do it for anything less. And he said for a movie company it was a bargain, it would cost them twice as much to build a reproduction, and there was something wrong with them if they couldn't spend such a small amount. I could see that nothing would change him. I know how stubborn a German can be."

"And I know you're a good bargainer," he said. "So that's what you're going to have to pay?"

"I told him I would have to talk to the producer. I shall have to talk to somebody. I told you, I am only a girl who works in an office. Perhaps with all my savings I can find ten thousand marks. I don't have rich friends. I was such a fool to think I could do this all by myself."

He gazed at her thoughtfully.

"So you'd like to go back to our old deal, and go Dutch again?"

"If you could forgive me. And you have the best right to share the treasure."

He shook his head callously.

"We still haven't found any treasure. But if you want to start again now, with me putting up four marks to your one, we're not fifty-fifty any more. We're eighty-twenty."

Her eyes swam before she covered them.

"All right," she said. "It's my own fault. But I can't come as close as this and give it all up. I accept."

"And I hope it's a lesson to you," he said virtuously. "But before I put up this dough, I'd like to see the house and be sure you've found the right one. That is, if you think you can trust me now not to burgle it on my own."

"I will show it to you whenever you like."

"Why not now?" said the Saint. "Pay for the drinks, and let's go."

They went out and took a taxi. She gave the driver directions in which he heard "St Pauli Hafenstrasse"; the route seemed at first to be heading towards the Reeperbahn again, but turned down towards the river and the docks. When they stopped and got out, he could see the spire of a small church, but it was not at all individual : almost any church with a steeple would have had some resemblance to the one in the map-drawing.

"It is just along here, on the Pinnasberg," Eva said.

There was no question about the house when he saw it. Although it was wedged into a single façade by its neighbours on either side, instead of standing alone, the complicated woodwork and the steep gabled roof capped with the unique round tower were exactly as he recalled them from the crude sketch he had seen the night before, even before Eva produced the parchment and unrolled it for him again under a street lamp.

"It certainly seems to fit," he admitted to her, and had to admit to himself a way-down tremor of excitement that was no longer such a frequent symptom to him as it had been in less hardened days.

"It does—even the distance and direction from the church. I measured them."

"What does all the writing say?"

"The first part tells where the house is. It seems easy to you now, of course, but it was not easy for me the first time to know where he was talking about. In five hundred years, there are many changes——Then it tells what to look for inside the house. The treasure is in one of the cellars which lead towards the river, in a closed-up tunnel. He gives all the measurements and the marks to follow."

Simon surveyed the edifice broodingly.

"I still say the rent is inflated," he remarked. "It might be much cheaper to burgle the joint."

"But then we would still have to dig. It would take more than just a few minutes, and suppose we were caught? The other way, we have plenty of time, two weeks, and nothing to worry about."

"Except fifty thousand marks," said the Saint. "Before we put our shirts on this, let's be certain there isn't any other way to swing it."

Without waiting for her compliance, he crossed the street and mounted the steps and hammered on the door of the house they had been looking at. She caught up with him before it opened.

"What are you going to do?"

"See if we can't make a better deal. Just introduce me as your boss the movie producer."

It was Franz Kolben himself who opened the door, for that was where he lived, and he had made it a most profitable residence since he took over the management from his father-in-law, with the help of such intermittent interruptions. Although he had not expected a visit at precisely that moment, he was quick to put on the curmudgeonly expression which it called for.

"Excuse me for disturbing you at such an hour," said the Saint, when Eva had made the necessary presentation, "but I must call Hollywood tonight and give them all the information."

"Come in," Kolben said grudgingly.

"You might be interested to know that the new star we're introducing in this picture is a German," Simon chattered on, once they were all inside the hallway and the street door was closed again. "I wonder if you'd recognize him."

He took from his pocket the card with a silhouette on it which was not his own, and showed it. Kolben scarcely batted an eyelid—but to Simon Templar a much more infinitesimal flicker of reaction than that would have been enough. Without an instant's hesitation, without even waiting for any verbal rejoinder, he brought his fist up under Kolben's helpfully extended chin in the shortest and wickedest uppercut in the business.

"Have you gone mad?" Eva gasped, as Kolben descended to the floor with the precipitate docility which the standard cliché compares with being poleaxed.

"That's what I'll have to try to sell the jury, darling, if I'm wrong about this," Simon answered; and as she suddenly flew at him he hit her reluctantly but accurately on the back of the neck with the minimum of essential force.

That gave him a few minutes with nothing to worry about except the chance that they might have other friends in the house; but as he sped swiftly and softly from room to room he found no one except, at last, trussed to an iron cot in an attic, the one man he had been seeking.

"Herr Roeding," he said reproachfully, as he was removing the cords and adhesive tape, "it's all right for you to poke around in antique shops and accept free guidebooks, but a research chemist of your age shouldn't escort young women to the hot spots of the Reeperbahn."

"They are all in it together," spluttered the victim. "Uhrmeister who gives out the books, his daughter who wants to see all the shows, the uncle who is a pawnbroker, and her husband who owns this house. And that story about Störtebeker's goblet——"

"I've heard it," said the Saint. "It's very well done. And if you'd been the ordinary sucker it would only have cost you a few thousand marks. But Koblen recognized you or your name, or both, and he must have realized that you were worth more on the hoof than as just another disappointed treasure-hunter. If a pal of ours in Washington hadn't asked me to give it a whirl before it was officially reported that you were missing and might have defected under the Wall, you would probably have been smuggled out on the next freighter to Russia."

Ernst Roeding massaged some colour back into his hands, but his face was still grey.

"Who are you?" he asked.

THE BIGGER GAME

BECAUSE I once translated the autobiography of Juan Belmonte, one of the historically greatest bullfighters of them all, with what I hoped was an authoritative introduction, Simon Templar has by association been assumed by some readers to be an *aficionado* himself, or even a graduate practitioner of the art. In one interview an English reporter, who had received disappointing replies to a few leading questions designed to show up the Saint's devotion to bullfighting, which could in print be either pilloried or ridiculed according to the delightful convention of most English interviewing, complained peevishly, "You sound so lukewarm about it—have you lost your *afición*?"

"I just haven't been in any of the countries where they do it, lately," said the Saint.

"And you don't miss it? I'd have expected a man like you to want to try it himself, like other people take up golf. Haven't you ever tried to stand up to a bull with a cape?"

"If I told you about my greatest moment in that line," said the Saint equably, "you'd either splash it all over your paper, which would be a breach of confidence, or you wouldn't believe me, which would hurt my pride. So let's save us both embarrassment by trying some other subject. After all, burglars can make just as big headlines as bullfighters."

In simple fact, Simon had tried his cape-work against very young bulls at round-up time on the *fincas* of a couple of breeders whom he had known in Spain, and his natural grace and superb reflexes had caused some of the privileged observers to proclaim perhaps extravagantly that he was a born phenomenon whose refusal to make it a career would be a disaster through which tauromachy would continue irreparably impoverished. But he had never taken any but a spectator's part in any formal *corrida*, and in spite of the assiduous journalist's imputation he had never felt any ambition to.

Nevertheless the Saint's last answer, like many of his smoothest evasions, was only a bald truth which it privately amused him to veil and confuse.

He did actually, once, make a *quite* such as no matador up to and including Belmonte ever dreamed of, or is likely to dream of since, except in nightmares.

(I must intrude myself again here to mention that what I have just italicized has no connection with the English word "quite", meaning "moderately", as in a phrase like "quite nice", often pronounced "quaite naice" : this one is pronounced in Spain something like *key-tay*, and in a formal bullfight refers to the work of luring the bull away from a fallen *picador*, the lancer on the horse which the bull has felled, despite the squeals of Anglo-Saxon tourists in the stands, who as charter members of some SPCA do not regard human beings as animals that should not be cruelly treated *Aficionados*, who may be more sentimental, rate the *quite* as a rather valiant job, sometimes almost heroic.)

Simon Templar really did think of the hunting of criminals sometimes as a sport, and infinitely more exciting than the pursuit of the much less cunning and dangerous quarry which satisfies other self-designated sportsmen. But just as devotees of the more generally accepted versions of the chase rate some forms as more

challenging than others, to the Saint one of the supreme
refinements was to spot the villain *before* he became the
answer to a whodunit, or to anticipate the crime before
the perpetrators had finally decided to commit it.

Sometimes, Simon maintained, a man is ineluctably
marked for murder. He may be the political candidate
with the reform platform in a town that doesn't want to
be reformed, the crook who has decided to squeal on a
powerful racket, the inconvenient husband who stands in
the way of somebody's hot ideas for a reshuffle—there
are many obvious possibilities. But since murders, like
marriages, require at least two participants, the consummation requires an inexorable aggressor as well as a
predestined victim.

There was an evening in London when the Saint felt
sure he had met both together. This was at the bar of
the White Elephant, which was a supper club where in
those days you might run into anyone that you read about
in the papers, and frequently did.

The slight swarthy man with the burning black eyes
and the ugly scar on one temple he recognized instantly
as Elías Usebio, who had been called the greatest matador
since Manolete : Simon had never seen him in the ring,
but that scimitar profile had been widely caricatured,
especially since his sensational wedding and equally
publicized retirement a year ago.

Iantha Lamb, whom he had married, or who had
married him, would have been ecstatically recognized by
many millions more to whom he was only a name which
they were still very vague about, such being the more
international scope of motion pictures and their attendant
publicity. Iantha Lamb was a movie star, if not of the first
magnitude, at least a luminary to gladden the box office.
Although there were sourpouts who sneered that she acted

better in bedrooms than before cameras, except for certain films which her first husband had spent a small fortune buying up, anything that she did was news and she had worked hard at making it newsworthy. Her assiduously advertised weakness was for men who lived with death at their elbow—racing drivers, lion tamers, deep-sea divers, test pilots, soldiers of fortune, young men on a flying trapeze, anyone whose luck had more chances to run out than that of most people. Her wild romances with these statistical bad bets had filled more columns of print than her thespian achievements ever earned, culminating with her marriage to Usebio, the *torero* who until he cut his pigtail had been generally rated most likely to become an obituary.

"You were sensational then, Elías," she said almost wistfully. "Nobody who hasn't seen you in a *corrida* can imagine how wonderful you were. Every time you stepped out into the ring, I died. But you always lived, and that was more wonderful still."

"And now I expect to go on living," Usebio said indulgently, "until I am knocked down on the sidewalk by a runaway bus."

"Does that mean that you lost your nerve?" asked the other man who was with them.

He was much taller and bigger, with the fine mahogany tan which develops on a certain type of Englishman, but as a rule only when he has been exiled for a long time to colonies where the sun shines more consistently than it normally does at home. He had large white teeth to contrast with his complexion, and an outdoor man's interesting crowfoot wrinkles to point up his light grey eyes, and the ideal dusting of grey in his hair to give it all distinction without making him seem old.

He too was recognizable—in a lesser degree, but Simon

happened to have read an article about him not long
before, in the kind of magazine one thumbs through in
waiting-rooms. His name was Russell Vail, and he was
what is rather oddly called a white hunter : that is, he
guided package-priced adventurers to the haunts of wild
animals, told them when to shoot, and finished off the
specimens that they wounded or missed, never forgetting
that a satisfied client must go home not only with a soporific supply of anecdotes but also with the hides, heads, and
horns to prove them. He had chaperoned a number of
Hollywood safaris into Darkish Africa and had written a
book about it, which made him a personality too.

"I only decided not to be stupid," Usebio said quietly.
"It is a matter of arithmetic. Even if you are very good,
every afternoon there is a chance for the bull to get you.
Each time you go out, he has more chances. If you shoot
at a target often enough, no matter how difficult it is, one
day you must hit it. Too many bullfighters have forgotten
that. They say, 'In one year, three years, when I am forty,
I will retire.' But before that, they meet a bull who does
not know the date. There is only one time when you can
say you retire and be sure of it. That is when you are
alive to say you will not fight again, not even once more."

"Quit while you're ahead, eh?" Russell Vail said
heartily. "Well, that's how the sharpies play cards."

"Elías was always very brave," Iantha Lamb said. "All
the critics always said that."

"So, I had been lucky, and I was well paid, and I had
not lived foolishly, as many bullfighters do. I was a rich
man. I did not have to go on fighting, except for a thrill.
And then I discovered a much greater thrill—to go on
living, and be the husband of Iantha. That was the surprise present I gave her on our honeymoon."

"And what a surprise," she said pensively. "The last

thing I ever expected. But don't blame it on me. I never asked for it."

Usebio looked up almost in pain, and said : "Who spoke of blame? I wanted to give you my life, and how could I give it if I did not have it?"

There was slightly awkward silence, and Russell Vail ordered another round of drinks.

Simon, who had been eavesdropping unashamedly, was suddenly aware of Iantha Lamb's huge slanting elfin eyes fixed on him with an intensity of the kind which every attractive male learns to interpret eventually, no matter how much modesty he may have started life with. He only met her gaze for a moment and then concentrated on stirring the ice in his Peter Dawson, but he could still feel her watching him.

Russell Vail took a hefty draught from his fresh glass and started up again.

"All this stuff about getting killed, Elías—honestly, aren't you making a bit much of it? Fox-hunters get killed. Football players get killed. House painters get killed. Even ordinary pedestrians get killed on the streets. Considering how many bullfighters there must be in Spain and Mexico, do they really have such a lot of accidents?"

"It is not the same," Usebio said patiently, though a sensitive ear could detect the underlying effort. "The fox is not trying to kill the hunter. The public does not want a house painter to come as close as he can to falling off his ladder."

"Oh, yes, your bullfight fans want their thrills. But even a fox has a more sporting chance. The bull *never* gets away, does he?"

"He is not intended to. It is so difficult to explain to an Anglo-Saxon. But bullfighting is not a sport. It is an exhibition, to let the matador show his skill and courage."

"By tormenting a wretched hunk of beef that's doomed before he starts?"

Vail smiled all the time, blazoning good nature with gleaming incisors.

"It is no more a hunk of beef than those African buffalo I have heard you speak of," Usebio said.

"But they aren't shut up in a little arena, either. They're out in the open, where I have to find them—and they're just as likely to be hunting *me* !"

"And you have a big gun that can knock them over with one touch of your finger." The ragged scar on Usebio's forehead seemed to throb lividly as he raised a finger to it, though his voice did not change. "Did you ever come close enough to one for it to do something like this to you?"

Vail took another solid sip, and answered a little more loudly : "I'm not so bloody silly. I'm not trying to impress an audience. But even without taking unnecessary risks, a lot of chaps in my profession have got themselves killed. A lot more than toreadors, I wouldn't mind betting."

Usebio winced.

"I do not know about toreadors, except what I have seen in a French opera, *Carmen.* The men who do what I do are called *toreros.*"

"All right, *toreros*—bullfighters—what's in a name?"

"Elías is being modest," his wife put in. "He's a *matador de toros*. That's more special than just any *torero*. It's like being a star instead of just any actor."

"I'm sorry," Vail said, smiling more relentlessly than ever. "No offence meant. But I'd still like to know the figures."

"Well, does either of you know them?"

There was no immediate answer, and Simon Templar could not resist sneaking another glance at the trio to

observe any non-verbal response. And once again, disconcertingly, the glance was trapped by Iantha Lamb's
boldly speculative gaze.

This time he couldn't break the contact too hastily
without looking foolish, and she said, while he was still
caught : "Somebody should be umpiring this—how about
you ?"

Simon felt four more eyes converging on him simultaneously, but they didn't bother him. He said amiably :
"I'm no statistician either."

"You don't look like one," she said. "You look much
more interesting. What are you ?"

That was one of the questions he always hated : the
truth was far too complicated for ordinary purposes, and
the easier falsehoods or flippancies became tedious after
all the times he had tried them.

"I've been called a lot of things."

"What's your name ?"

He decided that this was one situation where he might
as well give it, and let the gods take it from there.

It was perhaps significant, if not surprising, that
neither Vail nor Usebio had any reaction to it, other than
astonishment at the reaction of Iantha Lamb, who seemed
as if she would have been happy to swoon.

"My hero !" she crowed, while they looked understand-
ably blank.

"*Please*," begged the Saint, as she slid off her stool and
began to move towards him.

An expression of ineffable smugness came over her
internationally fabled face. She looked exactly like the
cat that had one paw on the mouse's tail.

"All right—for a price."

"Name it."

"Later," she said, in the husky undertone that had throbbed from a thousand sound tracks.

Possibly because of a linguistic advantage, Russell Vail was the first of her two escorts to recover.

"That's fine," he said, with unflagging joviality. "But can't we be introduced?"

She did that, formally. Usebio bowed with dignity. Vail shook hands, insisting on the grasp of his powerful paw.

"You must be something special," he said, "if you send Iantha like that." He might have been momentarily set back by the discovery that his consciously muscular grip was very gently but unmistakably equalled, but the check was barely perceptible. He went on, with the same geniality: "Did you ever do any big-game hunting?"

"A little," said the Saint.

"Do you know anything about bullfighting?" Usebio asked.

"A little."

"Well, what do you think?" asked Iantha Lamb.

Simon shrugged.

"I think you'll never settle that argument with figures, anyhow. So X number of guys were killed at the battle of Waterloo, and Y number of guys were killed at El Alamein. What formula do you use to figure who was braver?"

"In other words," she insisted, "the only proof would be to test one against the other, like making a bullfighter go big-game hunting, or sending a big-game hunter into a bullfight."

"I'd like to see any bullfighter take on a buffalo with his bare hands," muttered Vail. "Or a rogue elephant. Or——"

"Or a man-eating shark," Simon said. "Can both of

them swim? . . . I'm not being facetious. There are
different skills involved, as well as courage. A bullfighter
might be a lousy shot. A big-game hunter probably
wouldn't even know how to hold a cape. If you want to
match a bull-fighter and a big-game hunter on equal
terms—present company excepted, I hope—the only fair
way would be in some field where they're both amateurs."

Iantha Lamb pouted.

"What would you suggest?"

It was then perhaps that the Saint felt his first truly
premonitory chill. For an academic conversation, the
point didn't have to be pressed so hard. But he said
lightly: "How about tiddly-winks? It's easier to arrange
than shark wrestling."

She seemed petulantly disappointed, but Russell Vail
grinned more widely as he emptied his glass.

"That's a great idea," he said. "But I've got a better
one. Knives and forks and a juicy steak. Can we settle for
that? I'm famished."

While he and her husband competed amicably for the
bar bill, Iantha held the Saint with a stare of dramatic
malevolence which in spite of its obvious exaggeration
Simon felt was not entirely in fun.

"You don't get off so easily," she muttered. "I'm still
holding you to the bargain we made."

"Any time," said the Saint cheerfully.

"Where are you staying?"

"At Grosvenor House."

"Our table is ready," Usebio said, with rigid correct-
ness.

And that should have been the end of it, except for an
epilogue that Simon might have read in the papers, for it
was not the kind of situation that the Saint cared to
meddle in. The sometimes fatal by-products of sharp-

pointed triangles had crossed his path several times, but he did not seek them. Sometimes, however, they sought him.

He was finishing a rather late breakfast in his room the next morning when the telephone rang and a drowsy voice said: "Good morning. You see, I didn't forget."

"Maybe you're dreaming," he said. "You sound as if you were still asleep."

"I wanted to try and catch you before you went out. Are you busy for lunch?"

As he hesitated for a second, she said: "Or are you backing out this morning? Last night you said *any time*."

"I wasn't thinking of anything so daring and dangerous as lunch," he murmured.

She made a lazy little sound too deep to be a giggle.

"It still leaves the rest of the afternoon, doesn't it? Shall we make it the Caprice—at one?"

Somewhat to his surprise, she was punctual, and she had a fresher and healthier air than he had half expected. It was true that she wore too much makeup for daylight, for his taste, but that was not conspicuous in itself in one of the favourite lunching-grounds of London's show business. Even the Saint would have been less than human if he hadn't enjoyed the knowledge that he was observed and envied by a fair majority of the males in the restaurant.

"Gossip can't do me any harm," he remarked, "but did you think about it when you chose this place?"

"What could be more discreet?" she asked coolly. "If I'd suggested some cosy little hideaway, and anyone happened to see us there, they'd have something to talk about. But everybody meets everybody here—on business. It's so open that nobody wonders about anything."

"I see that you've studied the subject," he said respectfully. "And where is Elías?"

"Having lunch with a lawyer, in the sort of place lawyers go to."

"What kind of lawyer?"

She gave a short brittle laugh.

"About making a will. Not what you're thinking. Elías is a Catholic, of course. I'm not, but he's as serious as they make 'em. He couldn't ask for a divorce if I slept with his whole *cuadrilla* and broke a bottle over his head any time he came near me. When these Papists get married, they really mean 'till death do us part'."

Mario the presiding genius came to their table himself and said: "Did you ever try kid liver? It's much more delicate than calf's liver. I have a little, enough for two portions."

"I couldn't bear it," said Iantha, emoting. "A poor little baby goat! . . . I'll just have some vichyssoise and lamb chops."

"My heart bleeds for that poor little lamb," said the Saint. "I'll try the kid liver."

It was delicious, too, worthy of a place in any gourmet's memory; but he knew that she hadn't forced that meeting merely for gastronomic exploration.

"I suppose we're all inconsistent," he said, "but do you try to rationalize your choice of animals to be sentimental about?"

"Of course not. I just know how I feel."

"I suppose lamb is a meat, a kind of food you see in markets and restaurants. You don't associate it with a live animal. You're not used to eating goat, so you visualize it alive, gambolling cutely when it's young. But you don't think of fighting bulls as beef, and I don't expect you're used to eating lions."

"That's different. Lions and fighting bulls can kill you. So a man can prove something when he kills one. You should be an analyst—you've found my complex. There's something about danger and courage that gives me a terrific thrill."

"You'd've loved it in ancient Rome, with the gladiators."

"I might have."

"And when they killed each other, it would've been even more thrilling."

She bit her lip, but it was only a teasing play of little pearly incisors on a provocative frame of flesh.

"I've often wondered. I wish I could have seen it just once, for real, instead of in Cinemascope. I've always had this thing about brave men."

"Don't look at me. I'd like to be a coward, but I'm too scared."

"You don't have to make dialogue. I can be honest. You fascinate me. You always have, ever since I first read about you."

This was the moment of truth—to borrow a phrase from the clichés of tauromachy. The inevitable preliminary chit-chat had run its course, perhaps rather rapidly, in spite of the convenient restaurant punctuations for sampling and savouring. But now he was going to be cut off from the easier evasions. It was imminent in the velvet glow of her faintly Mongolian eyes.

He took a carefully copious sip of the *rosé* which he had ordered for their accompaniment—it was a Château Ste Roseline, delicately fruity, and an uncommon find in England, where the warm weather which fosters the appreciation of such summery wines is normally rarer yet.

"Tell me the worst," he said.

"I'd like to have an affair with you."

Simon Templar put down his glass with extreme caution.

"Does Russell Vail know about this?" he inquired.

"Yesterday I might have cared. Today I don't."

"But he kills lions. Even elephants."

"But you've killed *men*, haven't you?"

"Not for fun."

"But you have. And you will again—if someone doesn't do it to you first. That makes you bigger than either of them."

"I'm glad you brought in that 'either'," said the Saint. "Let's not forget your husband. Sometimes there's another angle on the 'till death do us part' bit, especially among Latins. Sometimes the husband provides the necessary death—and it isn't his own."

"Don't try to pretend that frightens you."

"Some things do. Like the idea that you must be serious."

"Because I don't make any bones about it? Life is too short. This is something I want, and I hoped you might like it too. Why not make it easy for you?"

It is of course well known to all readers of noble and uplifting fiction, if there still are any, that any self-respecting hero's response to such a proposition is to smack the tramp sharply on the rump and tell her to go peddle her assets elsewhere. But how much saintliness can be reasonably asked of anyone, when the tramp happens to be an Iantha Lamb?

"May I think it over?" said the Saint.

She nodded calmly.

"But don't think too long—I'm leaving for Rome next week to start a picture. Unless you're in a travelling mood."

He wondered long afterwards what decision he might

eventually have come to—he was not hidebound by any of the usual conventions, but there was something about the manner of her offer which reminded him uncomfortably of a decadent empress requesting the services of a vassal, a request that was almost a command and at the same time a favour. The impediment to reacting with proper indignation was that she actually was a kind of empress in the echelons of the twentieth century in which he was a kind of buccaneer, and her favour was an impossible pipe dream for which millions of men would have deliriously given everything that they owned. In all honesty, he sometimes thought that the only thing that stopped him from capitulating on the spot might have been an absurd reluctance to be the pushover which she had so many good reasons to expect.

More fortunately than he probably deserved, the dilemma was resolved for him that time at what could have been the last moment before it became crucial.

Two evenings later when he returned to Grosvenor House from the movie where he had finished the afternoon—it was a recent Iantha Lamb picture for which a billboard had caught his eye after lunch, and the curiosity of seeing it in this peculiar context had been too much for him—he found three telephone messages in his box recording attempts by Russell Vail to reach him during the day. The latest was time-stamped only minutes before, and Simon yielded to another curiosity and called the number it asked him to directly he got to his room.

"Glad I got you at last," boomed the hunter. "It's a bit late, I know, but I was hoping you could have dinner with us tonight. I mean, with Iantha and Elías. We all thought you'd make a good fourth."

Simon reserved the observation that only an Iantha Lamb would consider herself and three men a good foursome. The breezy tone of Vail's voice seemed to dispose of a possibility which he had been half prepared for when he returned the call, that Vail might have had the phantasmagoric notion of warning him that trespassing rights on Elías Usebio's marital property were already bespoke. He had nothing else planned; and seeing Iantha again under the maximum conceivable chaperonage might help, somehow, to produce a solution to the problem which he had been trying to ignore.

"That's nice of you," he said.

"Fine. Suppose we pick you up at seven."

"I'll be downstairs."

"Don't dress up. We thought we'd drive out to a place in the country."

"Suits me."

"And one other thing. Could you bring along some of your professional gear—I mean, something to pick a lock with?"

The Saint's eyebrows edged upwards.

"There's something funny about this telephone," he said. "It sounded exactly as if you said you wanted me to bring something to pick a lock with."

"I did."

"What sort of lock?"

"On a big iron gate. Don't worry—we're not going to steal anything. We'll explain it all later. But bring something. See you at seven."

Simon was waiting in the lobby when Vail came in, shook hands heartily, and looked around as if in search of some luggage that the Saint should have had with him.

"You didn't think I was joking about that lock, did you, old boy?"

Simon touched his breast pocket.

"If this gate isn't on a bank vault, I can probably handle it. If you've got a good reason."

"Later. I think it might appeal to you. But first, dinner."

In the back courtyard there was a shiny new Jaguar with Iantha Lamb at the wheel and a vacant seat beside her. As Simon approached it, he saw that Elías Usebio was already sitting in the back. The commissionaire opened the off-side front door with a flourish, and Vail nudged the Saint forward.

"The place of honour for the guest of honour," he said.

"No argument, old boy. That's the drill."

Simon had no desire to argue. He made himself comfortable beside Iantha, and hoped that her husband and Vail were equally relaxed in the back seat.

"Are you afraid of women drivers?" she asked, as they ploughed into the traffic complex of Marble Arch.

"Not so much when I'm on their side," he replied. "And when there's nothing to worry about but their own car—this *is* your own, I hope?"

"Elías just gave it to me the other day, to take to Rome. You notice it's built for driving on the right."

"I'm glad you've noticed that they drive on the left here," he said. "Elías might have to put off his retirement to buy another if you broke it up."

"*He* wouldn't, but I would. He's the rich one. He's earned a lot more than I have, and hardly spent a *peseta*."

"I was not brought up to treat money like old newspapers," said Usebio gently.

"Or to pay ninety per cent income taxes," retorted his wife.

They were heading north, and the car moved as if it

held the road only because it was perfectly disciplined, not because it didn't have the power to lift up and fly if it wanted to.

"Where are we going?" Simon inquired presently.

"St Albans, first," said Iantha.

He thought that over.

"They've got some Roman ruins there," he said, "but you'll see much better ones when you get to Rome."

"They've got a good pub, too, Russell says."

"Is it so exclusive that we have to break into it?"

"We'll tell you about the lock business afterwards," said Vail. "We'll give you a good dinner first, and then see if you feel like tackling it."

The pub was quaintly named The Noke, but it had the air of substantial serenity which the connoisseur of English hostelries recognizes at once. They had cold dry martinis in the pleasantly timbered bar, except for Usebio, who would take nothing stronger than St Raphaël. They ordered smoked salmon and roast grouse, which were excellent, as was the Château Smith Haut Lafitte which the proprietor suggested.

The conversation was brightly enjoyable but totally unimportant; only Usebio seemed a little apart and pre-occupied with serious private thoughts, though his rare responses were unfailingly courteous. It would have been a perfectly pleasant and unquoteworthy dinner party except for the enigma that went with it, the motivation under which Simon had been included, which nobody would refer to any more. He had to reach back deliberately for the first psychic hunch he had had, and remind himself that both the other men were dealers in death by training and vocation.

For Russell Vail, in the ultimate analysis, was only a kind of professional butcher glamourized by the fact that he used a rifle instead of an axe ; and the word *matador*, in Spanish, most literally means simply "killer". . .

Simon could only wait; and at last Vail paid the bill and they went outside. It was one of those cloudless summer nights that England can produce sometimes, in spite of her inclement reputation and the bad luck that dogs her meteorologists on the rare occasions when they venture to predict one, with a full moon that hung overhead like a stage lantern. Vail looked up at it with satisfaction, and said : "It couldn't be brighter in Kenya. Let's make the most of it."

As they approached the car, Iantha said to the Saint: "Would you like to drive ?"

Without waiting for an answer, she slipped into the other front seat. Simon got in behind the wheel, and moved his seat back.

"Where to ?"

"I'll have to look at the map."

She directed him out on A5, the highway historically known by the oddly prosaic name of Watling Street, which runs northwestwards across the countryside almost as straight as the proverbial crow's flight all the way to Shrewsbury, on foundations laid out by Roman surveyors in the days when Caesar's legions knew St Albans by the name of Verulamium. Simon bore down with his right foot, and the Jaguar responded in a way that reminded him of the mighty Hirondel which had been his beloved chariot in the young days of more uncomplicated adventure. But he was only able to enjoy that reminiscent exhilaration for a few minutes and half again as many miles before Iantha was warning him to slow down for a turning on the left. He saw the signpost as they swung into the secondary road, and had a wild preposterous presentiment that every sober habit of thought tried to reject.

But after a couple of more turnings in a couple of more crooked miles taken at more sedate speed, he knew that this was going to be a bad night for sober thinking when Russell Vail leaned forward behind him and said : "I think you'd better stop about here, old boy, wherever you can find a good place to park."

Simon brought the car to a stop, and said : "Is this where you want me to pick a lock ?"

"We're close enough. We'd better walk the rest of the way."

"To Whipsnade ?"

"You guessed it."

Whipsnade, it must be explained here for the benefit of readers who are not familiar with the British scene, is the pride of England's zoos—a park in which an assortment of animals acclimated from every continent on the globe roam in their suitably landscaped enclosures, behind bars and moats as tidily camouflaged as possible, from which sanctuaries they are privileged to study human beings in a semi-natural habitat.

The Saint did not move.

"I suppose it might be fun to steal a giraffe," he said. "But it'll be hard work getting it in this car."

"We aren't going to steal anything."

"Then you'll have to tell me what the game is, before we go any farther."

Elías Usebio stirred and said : "We are going to settle an argument—the argument we began the other night. He has challenged me to try my cape against any animal with horns that he will choose."

"And what does *he* do to prove anything?"

"I'll tackle anything with claws that Elías chooses, just using a native spear," answered Vail.

"And I thought there ought to be an impartial umpire,

like when we picked you at the White Elephant," said Iantha. "Besides, we couldn't think of anyone else who could get us in."

For a few seconds Simon Templar was silent. The idea was as outrageous as anything he had ever heard, but that was not enough to take his breath away. Contemplated as a pure spectacle, it was an invitation that no epicure of thrills could have refused. The impudence of the assumption that he would be a party to its illicit procurement he could shrug off. He hesitated only while he thought of the reasons why it might be an honest and Saintly duty to put a stop to the whole project; and in the same space of time he realized absolutely that the contest would be decided sometime, somewhere, with or without him, and that the best thing he could do was to be there.

"All right," he said. "But we can't do it by the front gates."

"You mean *you* can't?" said Vail, in the jovially disparaging tone which he used so masterfully, which almost dared you to reveal yourself such a lout as to take offence. "And I've heard you were the greatest cracksman since Raffles."

"I'm better," Simon said calmly. "But the main entrance would just be stupid. There are keepers' cottages all around there. The only animals we'd be likely to get near would be watchdogs."

"There speaks the expert. But I'm sure he'd know how to cope with the problem."

"I was there once, years ago," said the Saint slowly. "I remember that on the far side of the grounds, that would be to the northeast, there were some enclosures that ran downhill, and you could walk around them, and then you were outside on a long slope with a fine view but only fields and pastures between you and a road I could see at the bottom. I think, since we've got to walk anyhow, if we found that road, there wouldn't be much to stop us hiking up the hill and into the back of the park."

Iantha handed him the map, and he studied it under the dashboard light.

Then he drove on again.

Nobody spoke another word before he stopped a second time. He got out and studied the skyline over a gate.

"This ought to do it," he said.

Usebio opened the trunk of the car and took out a folded bundle of cloth, and a short leaf-bladed spear which he handed to Vail. Simon unlatched the gate, and they followed Iantha through.

It was a steady climb of about three-quarters of a mile over rough grass. Simon set a pace which was intentionally geared to his estimate of the legs of Usebio, whom he didn't want to exhaust before his trial; he figured that no exertion of that kind should bother Vail. Iantha Lamb, who had worn a loose peasant skirt and flat-heeled shoes which he now realized must have been chosen less for modest simplicity than in shrewd preparedness for any eventuality, kept up without complaining. They negotiated three wire fences on the way, without much difficulty: after the first fifty yards, the moonlight seemed bright enough for a night football game.

Then presently it was not so bright as they approached the black shadows of the trees and shrubbery that capped the last acres of the rise; and suddenly, startlingly close, belled out a fabulously guttural warning that reverberated in the deepest chords of the human fear-instinct.

"A lion," Russell Vail whispered lightly. "We picked a good guide."

"I got you in," said the Saint. "Now you take over."

In a moment they were on a narrow road, one of the

painlessly macadamized trails on which safaris of short-winded suburbanites and their spoiled progeny were permitted, for an additional fee, to cruise among the fauna in their own little cars.

"I know where I am now," said Vail. "I came up this morning to look around."

He led them briskly along the road and then off to the right on another path that branched off it. The going was slower for a while under the shade of some trees and presently of a building from which came the grunts and rustlings of unseen beasts; then quite soon they were in the open again, and next to them was a fence of massive timber. The fence enclosed a very uncertain oblong about a hundred yards in its greatest length and half of that at its widest, on one side of which was an equally massive rough-hewn structure like a stable.

And standing out in the full glare of the moon, rotund, enormous, glistening, primeval, motionless, but evidently sensing their presence, was the animal.

Vail waved his hand towards it.

"There you are, Elías," he said. "Let's see what you can do with him."

"A rhinoceros," Iantha breathed.

"A beauty. Just arrived last week, and still not housebroken."

"But that isn't——"

"It has horns," Vail pointed out. "Two of 'em. You can see 'em from here. Just arranged tandem, instead of sideways like a bull. That might even make it easier. But it fits the terms of the dare. Of course, if Elías is scared to take it on . . ."

The matador stood looking at it, as immobile as the monster itself. The moonlight could not have shown any change of colour, and his thin hawk's face was like a mask of graven metal in which the eyes gleamed like moist stones.

Then he climbed carefully over the barrier and began to walk slowly forward, opening his cape.

In the stillness, Simon could hear the breathing of his companions.

The rhinoceros allowed Usebio to advance several yards, with its glinting porcine stare turned directly towards him. Simon thought he had read somewhere that rhinos were near-sighted, but if so this one had certainly caught a scent that told it which way to look. Yet it stood for seconds like a grotesque prehistoric relic, with no movement except a stiffening of its absurdly disproportionate little piggy tail.

Usebio stopped with his feet together, turned partly sideways, and spread the cape, holding it up by the shoulders, in the classic position of citing a bull.

And with a snort the rhino exploded into motion.

Its short chunky legs seemed to achieve no more than an ungainly trot, but the appearance was deceptive. There was barely time to realize what an acceleration it generated before it was right on top of Usebio. And Usebio stood his ground, turning harmoniously with the cape and leading the brute past him, gracefully but a little wide.

Iantha gasped, almost inaudibly.

The rhino blundered on a little way, turning in an astonishingly tight circle, and charged again. And again Usebio led it past him, a trifle closer, as if its nose were magnetized to the cloth, in a formal *verónica*.

The rhino scrambled around again, it seemed even faster, and launched itself at the lure a third time without a pause.

And suddenly Iantha Lamb screamed, a small sharp cry as if something clammy had touched her.

It may have been that Usebio started to turn his head at the sound, or that it only divided his concentration for a fractional instant; certainly he was trying to work still closer to his animal, and he had not yet perfectly judged or adapted himself to the dimensions of a three-ton beast that was as broad as a boat. He carried the horns and the head safely past him, but it caught him solidly with its shoulder and flung him aside much as the fender of a speeding truck might have done. He fell eight feet away and lay still with his face in the dirt.

There are things that happen in decimals of the time that it takes to report or read them. Like this :

Simon looked at Vail and said : "Your cue ?"

Vail showed his teeth and said : "Not me, old boy. I only bet I'd take on claws."

Simon grabbed the spear with one hand and smashed Vail's lips against his teeth with the other.

Vail stumbled back, falling.

Iantha's face was enraptured.

Simon vaulted the rails, and came down running.

And all that had happened while the rhinoceros hesitated imperceptibly over renewing its assault on an object that had become limp and prostrate.

Then it caught sight of the Saint racing towards it, yelling insanely, and found a more interesting target for its fury. With a slobbery *whroosh!* it veered to meet him.

Simon tried the trick that he had seen *banderilleros* use when planting their darts in a bull during their phase of the fight. He swerved a little to his right, Usebio and the fallen cape being to his left; and then at the last moment that he dared he dug in his heels and broke back diagonally to the left, at the same time hurling the spear towards the oncoming rhino's left jowl. The point could have made no more than a pinprick in the pachyderm's vulcanized hide, but it added its distraction to the surprise of the Saint's change of course, and the behemoth thundered by him with a momentum that even its own colossal power needed time to check.

In that dreadfully evanescent respite the Saint reached the cape, snatched it up, and spread it as he had been taught to do by friendly *toreros* at the testing of calves. In the one sideways glance that he could spare, he saw Usebio rolling over and struggling to rise up on his hands and knees.

"*A la barrera!*" Simon shouted, and went on in Spanish, which would most clearly penetrate Usebio's daze: "I will keep him off. But hurry!"

Then the rhino was bearing down on him like an express train. He would not have apologized for the cliché. It seemed to shake the earth like the biggest locomotive that ever ran on rails. But somehow he led it past him with the cape, not stylishly, but as best he recalled the movement.

It lurched and grunted and skidded around and came again. And again he made it follow the cloth instead of his body.

If Iantha Lamb had screamed again he would have laughed without a flicker of his eyes.

But he did get a glimpse of Usebio crawling painfully but with increasing strength towards the fence, and knew that he hadn't misinterpreted the collision which had felled the matador. Usebio had only been winded by a glancing blow, perhaps with a couple of cracked ribs, but nothing worse. If he could only get out of the corral.

Three, four, five, six more times the Saint gave his best simulated *verónicas* to a rampaging homicidal quadruped which whirled and came back for more with a terrifying swiftness and relentless persistence that even the bravest Andalusian bull never matched. But neither would his technique and configurations have brought *olé's* from the captious critics in the *Plaza de toros* at Seville. This was a reproach that Simon had no leisure to fret about. He was busy enough keeping the most mean-tempered *Diceros africanus* that ever had the privilege of an introduction to European culture from eviscerating him with one of its anachronistic horns.

Somehow he was able to keep the performance going until Usebio had rolled under the low bar of the stockade, safely to one side of the segment towards which Simon was baiting the rhino, until he knew everything was all right and he shamelessly dropped the cape over its head and sprawled over the top banister just as his paleolithic playmate crashed into the posts like a berserk baby tank.

There were many more people outside than he had left there—men in uniforms and parts of uniforms and other clothes. He had been distantly aware of their arrival during his last passes but had been far too occupied to take much note of it.

"What d'you think you're doing?" demanded the ranking one unnecessarily.

"Settling a silly bet," Simon replied placatingly. "I know it was naughty of us, but there's no harm done."

The keeper turned his flashlight from Usebio, who was now standing up brushing off his clothes, to Vail, who was dabbing his mouth with a red-stained handkerchief.

"Oh, no? What about him?"

"He slipped trying to get over the fence first, when he saw the other fellow in trouble. It's nothing serious."

The beam swung on to Iantha Lamb and rested there, and someone sucked in his breath sharply.

"Why, isn't that———"

"Yes, it is," said the Saint. "And I'm sure you wouldn't want to get her a lot of bad publicity. Now if we made up to you for the trouble we've given you, couldn't we forget the whole thing?"

There was no conversation whatever on the way back to town, after Simon had walked down the hill and brought the car around to the main entrance. Iantha drove, again with the Saint beside her, though he had tried to offer the seat to Usebio.

"No," said the matador. "I shall be quite comfortable. The front is better for you, with your long legs."

He said nothing about the long legs of Russell Vail. He may have felt instinctively that it would be diplomatic not to make Vail and the Saint sit together, though he had asked no questions about Vail's puffy mouth. And Vail seemed to think it best not to reopen the subject in front of Usebio.

"You can drop me off at my sister's," Vail said, as they came down Abbey Road, and Iantha obviously knew where that was. Vail got out and said: "Good night. I'll call you tomorrow." He looked in at the Saint and said: "I hope I see you again soon."

"Any time," said the Saint, exactly as he had once said to Iantha.

She drove to Claridge's, and Usebio said: "I will get out, but you must take Mr. Templar home."

"Nonsense," said the Saint. "I'll get a taxi. Or I'd just as soon walk. She has to take care of you."

"To that, I say nonsense," said Usebio. "I am all right. Only a few bruises. I will sit in a hot bath and tomorrow I am all right. It is nothing like a *cornada*." He was out of the car already, and put his hand in at Simon's window. "I insist. Tonight you saved my life. Is it so much to take you home? *Va con Diós, amigo.*" The thin lips smiled coldly, but the dark eyes glowed like hot coals. "You would have made a good bullfighter. You understand what is *pundonor*."

The Jaguar pulled away, and Simon Templar leaned back at the fullest length that his seat would let him.

"Do you understand what is *pundonor*?" she asked at length.

"It's a sort of romantic-chivalric concept of an honour that's bigger than just ordinary honour, or honesty," he said very quietly and remotely. "A sort of inflexible pride that would make you go through with a bet to dive off the Brooklyn Bridge even after you found out that the East River was frozen solid."

She said: "Or that would make you try to live up to your reputation because a hero was needed, and there was nobody else around?"

"Russell isn't a coward," said the Saint. "Don't sell him short."

"Then why didn't he fight you after you hit him?"

"Because it was safer to be consistent, and go on looking like someone who couldn't have helped Elías. Why did you scream?"

"I couldn't help it. Something touched me, and with all those jungle creatures around I naturally thought of snakes, and——"

"And that was all you could think of."

"Russell must have goosed me."

The Saint sighed.

"It's possible. I wouldn't ask him, because he'd deny it anyhow. But somebody must have wanted Elías to die. It was thrilling, wasn't it?"

"You were wonderful."

"*Morituri te salutamus*—we who are about to die salute

you. I think I said you were born in the wrong century. And if Elías had been killed, Russell and I could have fought it out. And if I killed him, some day some new young upstart would be challenging me. Just like the cave men."

They turned into the Grosvenor House courtyard off Park Street, and she braked the Jaguar and said: "Ask me in."

"I'm sorry," he said. "I don't want to be one of your gladiators."

In one smooth movement he was outside the car and she was staring out at him like a perplexed and perverse pixie.

"Nobody," she said in a low unbelieving voice—"nobody ever turned me down."

"That's why I'll be the one man in your life that you'll never forget," he said wickedly. "And there's one other thing I want you to remember."

"What's that?"

"It's none of my business how you work out your personal problems with Elías. But if I ever hear of him having a fatal accident, it had better be very convincing. Or you can be sure that whatever the jury says, I shall take the trouble to arrange another accident for you. Please never forget that—darling."

He blew her a kiss off his fingertips, and smiled, and walked into the hotel.

THE CLEANER CURE

S<small>IMON</small> T<small>EMPLAR</small> suffered neither fools nor pests gladly, but he was never too stubborn to admit that even the most obnoxious person could have something to offer him that might be useful at some remote time in some odd way.

He did not like Dr. Wilmot Javers, whom he met at a cocktail party in London for which the occasion has no bearing on this story, but he talked with him. Or, rather, he listened and made a few conventionally encouraging noises while Dr. Javers talked.

"I came across a case recently that would interest you," Dr. Javers stated, in a tone that defied contradiction. "I said to myself at the time, this would be one for the Saint."

"Did you?" responded the Saint politely.

"Of course, I never dreamed I'd have the chance to find out whether you could solve it. But now you'll have to show me whether you're as clever as they say you are."

"I couldn't be," Simon responded promptly.

But Dr. Javers was not to be diverted. As a medico, he may have been extremely competent and conscientious, sympathetic and indefatigable in affliction, dedicated to his profession and his patients; but as an individual he was one of those opinionated and aggressive types that can only assert themselves by reducing somebody else.

There are physical specimens of the same mentality who, with a certain reinforcement of alcohol, upon spotting a former or even current boxing champion in a bar, are impelled to try their best to pick a fight with him—an occupational hazard of which every career pugilist is

acutely aware. What can they lose? If he declines the
challenge, he is yellow. If the loud mouth can score with a
sneak punch, he can boast about it for ever. But if the pro
gives him the beating that he deserves, then the champ is
nothing but a big bully picking on a poor helpless amateur. Even actors who portray tough-guy parts before
movie or TV cameras, merely to support their wives and
children, are the recurrent targets of hopped-up heroes
who feel inspired to prove that these actors are not as
tough as the script makes them.

The Saint was exposed to this psychosis on two planes—
not merely the physical, but also the intellectual, which in
several ways was harder to cope with, requiring more
patience than muscular prowess. But he had learned to
roll with the abstract punches as well as the other kind.

"Here's the situation," said Dr. Javers. "The subject is
a man thirty-eight years old, married, two children, more
than averagely successful in business. Never had a serious
illness in his life, but is somewhat overweight. His business
calls for a lot of expense-account wining and dining. His
only trouble is that the wining is often too much for him.
He isn't an alcoholic, and he holds it like a gentleman,
but he goes to bed drunk two or three nights a week,
regularly. I mean, when he lies down, it's a fine question
whether he falls asleep or passes out."

"So?"

"One night, after taking a foreign buyer out to dinner
and a couple of night clubs, he comes home and goes to
bed in his dressing room, as he always does when he's out
late. His wife is an understanding soul, and she doesn't
wait up for him. The next day, he has the usual hangover,
only it's much worse than usual."

"Must have been an extra big night."

"He has the splitting headache and the nausea, of

course, but much worse than he can ever remember having them. And a bad cough, though he can't remember whether he smoked a lot more than his normal quota of cigarettes. Naturally, he has no appetite for breakfast. But he doesn't improve during the day. He feels worse all the time, he can't eat, and his eyeballs turn yellow. The following day, his wife thinks he must have an attack of jaundice, and calls me in. By that time he has stopped passing urine. I do what I can, but in two days he is dead."

"Another casualty to the expense-account system," said the Saint. "His wife ought to sue the Government for instituting a tax system that forces business men to entertain each other to death just so they can have a little fun with their own profits before the tax collectors grab for them."

Dr. Javers frowned. It was evident that on top of everything else he disapproved of flippancy, at least when it detracted from the importance he attributed to his own conversation.

"I'd given him a complete check-up only three weeks before. His social-business drinking hadn't been going on long enough to do any irreparable damage. His liver and kidneys were still in good shape. He showed no signs of any cardiac condition. In fact, I would have testified anywhere that there was nothing organically wrong with him."

"Anyone can make a mistake, I suppose."

"Not me, Mr. Templar. Not that bad a mistake. In fact, to protect my own reputation, it was I who urged that there should be a post-mortem. The subject's wife agreed, and I was completely vindicated. He had absolutely no chronic lesion or disease. If he had watched his diet, cut down his drinking, and taken a little exercise, there was no reason why he couldn't have lived as long as any of us. But he died, actually, of acute kidney failure."

"So he was poisoned."

"Obviously. But what with?"

"I don't know. I didn't do it."

"I'll give you a little help. It was done with something that anyone can buy without any restriction, which you'd be likely to find in almost any house, and which isn't generally considered poisonous at all. And generally speaking, it isn't. This poisoning was a freakish accident. It depended on an entirely separate circumstance which I included in my summary, if you were paying close enough attention."

Simon made a heroic effort to mute a sigh.

"I'm no toxicologist, doctor," he said. "You tell me."

"I'll give you one more clue," Javers said, with visibly expanding egocentric glee. "There was a heavy smear of lipstick on the collar of the coat he had worn on his last night out. But he insisted, and I believe him, that this was merely a souvenir of the floor show at one of the clubs to which he had taken his customer, which had one of those numbers where the chorus girls make fools of some of the men at the ringside tables."

The Saint shrugged.

"I give up."

Javers shook his head, and his round smug face shone with delight. In any sensibly ordered world, no further justification should have been needed for punching him in the nose.

"Oh, no, you don't," he said. "You still haven't really tried. I want to find out how good you are. Think it over for a while."

He moved away, chortling to himself, leaving Simon

unexpectedly unhooked and joyfully free to set a course towards a prettily moulded blonde in another corner whom he had been wistfully watching for some time.

Needless to say, the Saint did not think about Dr. Javers's conundrum for a moment; but Dr. Javers was not so easily dismissed. An hour later he came all the way across the room to buttonhole Simon relentlessly again.

"Have you found the answer yet?"

"No," Simon said patiently. "What is it?"

The doctor beamed at him gloatingly.

"You haven't concentrated on it yet. I know, I've been watching you. Unfortunately I have to leave now, but I'm not letting you off so lightly. I'm going to leave you with the problem. It'll torment you later, when you're trying to go to sleep or waking up in the morning. And when you can't stand it any longer, you can call me." He handed Simon a card. "We'll have a spot of dinner together and I'll explain it to you. Or if you happen to have hit on that solution, I've got a few other scientific puzzles for you to sharpen your wits on. I expect I'll hear from you one of these days."

He departed again, chuckling fatly; and Simon put the card in his pocket and took a mental pledge never to look at it again or to waste another instant wondering what chemical coincidence Dr. Javers's patient could have succumbed to.

Experience should long since have taught him the intrinsic danger of such rash resolutions, but he felt that in this case at least there was nothing he could obtain from such an odious bore that would be worth the tedium and irritation of getting it. He held firmly to this erroneous assumption for several weeks, during which he was fully occupied with other matters that are recorded elsewhere in these annals, which left him no spare time to fret over tricky puzzles that did not immediately concern him.

The nudge of Destiny was still far from perceptible at first, one night in Paris when he came home very late to his suite at the George V, giving a perfunctory *bonsoir* to the anonymous cleaning woman whom he passed on her knees in the corridor. But he had hardly taken off his coat and tie when there was a timid touch on the buzzer at the outer door, and he opened it and recognized her more by her drab fatigue uniform than anything else.

"May I speak with Monsieur a moment?" she asked nervously.

"But certainly, *Madame*," he replied cordially, in the same French, giving her the ceremonious title which Gallic gallantry may accord even to the humblest servant.

She came in, a grey woman toil-worn to nothing but skin and bones and indefatigable persistence, yet with a great dignity in her large deep-set eyes.

"I know who you are, Monsieur Templar," she said, when she had shut the door. "Everyone talks about *le Saint* staying here. I have waited many nights for the chance to catch you at a good moment."

"What is your trouble?" he asked.

"It is a long story, but I will try to make it short. My name is Yvonne Norval. I had a husband once, and his name was Norval, so that is also the name of my daughter Dénise. But he died long ago, in Algeria, after the Liberation, which did not settle everything for the professional soldiers. Dénise is almost sixteen now, and she was born the day after I was notified of his death."

"A small consolation, perhaps. But it must have been hard for you to bring her up alone."

"Very hard, Monsieur. The pay of a French sergeant is not much, at the best, and the pension of his widow is even less. But we had waited a long time for a child, always promising ourselves that if ever we were blessed with one it should have the best upbringing that we could give it, at any sacrifice. For neither of us had had much, but there must always be a time when any family can improve itself, if the parents are determined to pass on to their children a little more than they received. And after I had lost my husband, this hope became an obsession. I was already twenty-seven years old when Dénise was born : I had had the best of my own life. But I still had a good figure and a pretty face, though you would not believe it now."

It was hard to realize that simple arithmetic made her no more than forty-three. Anyone's guess would have pegged her at least twelve years older. But the Saint said : "On the contrary, *Madame*, one sees that you must once have had great beauty, and now it has only matured, like a good wine."

"I had, at any rate, something that men still wanted, for a little while," she said calmly. "And since I no longer had any use for it, I gave the benefit to Dénise."

"*Je vous écoute*," said the Saint. "Please sit down. At an hour like this, I have nothing but time."

This was a poetic exaggeration, but on this occasion he did not feel that the time was wasted.

The tale that he heard might have sounded to a cynic like the plot for a soap opera that no soap manufacturer would dare to sponsor, but it was told with a stoical dispassionateness that gave it a quality of classic tragedy.

Yvonne Norval had chosen the oldest profession with no illusions, solely on her coldblooded estimate that there was no other in which she was qualified to earn so much money so quickly. But unlike most of her sisters in it, she had hoarded every franc that she could. She spent nothing on personal luxuries, and no more than the essential minimum on such decorative vanities as were necessary to attract her clientele; her spartan willpower and singleness of purpose substituted for the expensive stimulus of drink and drugs which many others depended on to numb their self-disgust; and with the cunning and ferocity of a tigress she evaded or fought off the approaches of the pimps who would have helped themselves to the largest share of her income. She did not say it all in those words, but the facts were implicit in her own austere way of telling it.

In seven years of this rigorous dedication, she had expended the last saleable vestige of her original stock-in-trade, but she had accumulated a fund that would guarantee her daughter's care and education for the next ten, on a much higher level even than she could have hoped for if a *fellagha* sniper's aim had been a little less deadly.

She placed the child in a convent school of excellent standing, representing herself as the widow of an Army officer whose snobbish family had sternly refused to recognize their marriage or its offspring. Too proud to plead for the charity of these intransigent in-laws, she was depositing everything he had left her to prepay the raising of their daughter in the style to which she should be entitled : the fact that she herself would thus be forced to take any menial job for her own subsistence was not to cloud the childhood of Dénise. When the little girl became aware enough to ask why Yvonne visited her so seldom and never took her home, she would be told that her mother was married again, to a man who was so intensely jealous of the past that he refused ever to see the fruit of it; perhaps one day he would relent, her mother was working on him constantly, but the day had not dawned yet. The sympa-

thetic nuns had agreed to lend their silence to the decep-
tion.

"They would have needed a very tolerant confessor
themselves," said the Saint, "if they had not been moved
by such a sacrifice as yours. But after this, did you still
have more trouble?"

"Like you, Monsieur, I thought it was ended. But if it
had been, I should not be talking to you. Instead, it was
only beginning. After all, there was a *maquereau* I did not
escape."

His given name was Pierre, and in the half-world
where he belonged he was known as Pierrot-le-Fût—a
gross arrogant beast of the type that are loosely called
Apaches, but not because there is anything noble in their
savagery. Of surnames he had a variety; but once when he
was picked up in a police dragnet it had amused him to
call himself Pierre Norval—that same day, Yvonne had
refused his "protection" for the nineteenth time, in particularly graphic phrases, and under the influence of a
stolen bottle of Calvados it had struck him as a brilliantly
subtle retaliation. Even afterwards, he was still entranced
with his own malicious genius, and continued to use the
name, grumbling obscure crudities about his unfaithful
"wife".

In a psychological reaction that has afflicted many better men, rejection had not quenched his interest but had
inflamed it. He did not think for an instant that she was
irresistible or irreplaceable, he knew a dozen girls who
were prettier or better built or more entertaining, but
that abstract estimate made it an even more intolerable
affront to his vanity that Yvonne should turn him down.
It had become a point of honour that he must subjugate
her, so that in his own time he could humiliate her as she
had humiliated him. And to this objective he had devoted

more tenacity and ingenuity than he would ever have squandered on any legitimate enterprise.

And when he finally found the key, it fitted more perfectly than he could have hoped for in his most vindictive imaginings.

"Somehow, he found out what I had done with Dénise, and how I had paid the school so that she would be safe no matter what became of me. Naturally, I had let no one know about the money I was saving. And now there was no way for him to touch it. But he had armed himself with the one weapon that I could not fight. He told me that unless I became his slave, he would wait until Dénise was old enough to be destroyed, and then tell her all the truth about herself and about me."

For a few seconds the Saint was utterly at a loss for words, and in that silence he realized that no comment he could have made would have been adequate. In a lifetime that had been lived as close as possible to every form of evil, he had never heard a blackmail threat of such callous enormity.

Finally he said: "You should have killed him."

"You are right. But that is easier for most people to say than to do, especially for a woman. And if I had done that, even the nuns might have turned against me. The whole scandal might have come out. And even if I escaped the guillotine, I could no longer have hoped to help Dénise a little more, perhaps, after she left the school—to see her sometimes and perhaps not have her hate me altogether for giving her up to satisfy the new jealous husband I had invented."

"So you had to accept Pierrot-le-Fût."

"Yes. I accepted him. I had a little time left in which men of a lower class, or drunk enough, would still pay for me. And even after that, he would not let me go. He had not yet satisfied his hate. He kept me as his cook, his servant, to wait on his friends and their girls and to clean up after them. And to bring home enough money to pay for this privilege, I could go out and work as a scrub woman also, as you saw me tonight."

Simon thought this must be the end of the story.

"You have my sympathy and my homage, *Madame*," he said. "But that cannot be all you wanted of me. Tell me what you think I could do."

"I would not have troubled you, Monsieur Templar, if only what I have been doing was enough. I am used to the work now, and to the beatings when he is drunk, and I am still able to hold back a little money which he does not know about, which I am saving for when Dénise will need it. But now, Pierrot threatens something much worse than before."

"Can there be such a thing?" asked the Saint incredulously.

"Yes. Now this filthiness says that what I do is no longer enough. He has been watching Dénise. She is old enough and pretty enough, he says, to profit him much more than I can, in the one trade that he understands."

Simon Templar would never again claim that he had heard everything.

"But what threat could he use to make *that* possible?"

"He may not need one. He can find some way to shame her at the school, by telling the truth about me to her, or to her friends, or to their parents. Then, when she is an outcast, by them or by her own shame, he will take over, by force if necessary. He and his kind know only one art, but they know it well. And because I tried so hard to have her gently brought up, she will have none of the defences that I had. Pierrot-le-Fût is not stupid, you must understand, but he is utterly ruthless, and he is obsessed with one idea which has become a mania. For him to reduce and ruin Dénise would be his last and greatest triumph."

"And, of course, there is no bribe left to offer him. He has had the satisfaction of making you suffer the last possible indignity. Now he can only look forward to the sadistic climax of proving that all your sacrifice was in vain."

"*C'est ça.* One believes, now, that the Saint understands everything."

"That's one thing I'll never do," said the Saint. "But I'll keep trying."

He lighted a cigarette and stared out of the elaborately lace-curtained windows through which he could see practically nothing, listening to the vague rumbles and beeps and blended voices and sporadic clatters of the city without hearing them, and wondered if some miracle would ever earn him a reprieve from the reputation to which he had dedicated himself.

He could no longer have been flippant about soap operas, but he was beginning to think that a magnificent soap opera could have been built around him, except that hardly anyone would have believed the plot material except himself.

"Tell me some more about this charmer, Pierrot-le-Fût," he said.

The details he was mainly interested in were the haunts and habits of the specimen. He wrote down certain addresses that Yvonne Norval gave him, and when he had finished asking questions she stood up with quiet dignity.

"I apologize for taking so much of your time, Monsieur," she said. "But since you have heard it all, may I dare to hope a little?"

"I will try to think of something," he said. "But whatever happens, when you leave this room, you must forget that you ever spoke to me, or told me anything. This may be our last meeting; but in any case, we never met."

"*C'est entendu, Monsieur le Saint.*"

It was the most natural thing for him to offer his hand as he opened the door for her, but he was somewhat stunned and embarrassed when she bent over it and touched it to her lips. Then, before he could protest, she was gone.

It was quite a while since the Saint had tackled such a relatively basic and elementary problem as this. Regardless of the visions of starry-eyed spiritual or psychological idealists, he had never believed in the redemption or rehabilitation of such creatures as Pierrot-le-Fût: he believed in one fast, thrifty, and final cure for what ailed them, a treatment which eliminated all risk of a relapse. The fact that he had not administered this remedy so often of late was not due to any loss of faith in the efficacy of death as a disinfectant, but to the distracting pressure of too many more intriguing and more profitable claims on his attention. He realized now how much he had missed some of the old simple pleasures. But it had taken a pustule of such almost incredible stature as Pierrot-le-Fût to remind him of them.

The next evening he headed for the area near Montmartre which was frequented by the self-baptized Pierre Norval and his ilk, not to sample any of the garish *boîtes* clustered around the Place Pigalle where pilgrims from all over the world pay their traditional respects to the symbols of mammalian reproduction, but to sift through some of the unglamorous outlying cafés where the parasites on the by-products of this activity meet to scheme, drink, boast, connive, gamble, and trade every kind of illicit merchandise—vegetable, mineral, and human. And without any elaborate disguise, using only a few of those subtle shifts of dress and demeanour which were his own inimitable masterpieces of camouflage, he was able to do it without ever incurring the kind of attention that would have greeted an ordinary tourist who had strayed so far from the time-honoured tourist trap-line.

He found Pierrot-le-Fût quite quickly, at the third of the addresses he had jotted down, an unattractive *bistro* off the Boulevard Clichy, and without evident nausea he sipped some extraordinarily foul and bitter coffee while he browsed slowly and exhaustively through the same edition of *Match* that he had mauled through each of the other stops he had made.

His purpose at that time was no more vital than to satisfy a student's curiosity to observe this excrescence with his own eyes, to verify certain aspects which Yvonne Norval's prejudice might have distorted, and to make a few observations of his own, in much the same way as a professional executioner discreetly assesses the weight and musculature of the man he is to hang.

Pierrot-le-Fût was a big man, built somewhat along the lines of the barrel which was only one of the possible meanings of his sobriquet; but in spite of his tubby shape he also looked hard as a cask is hard. He had small piggy eyes and a sadistic mouth from which a loud voice blustered mechanical obscenities. He had a flushed face and an equally ruddy nose which bespoke other habitual intemperances. He drank cognac from a large glass which was frequently refilled, and although it did not seem to be having any devastating effect on him at the time, this was still early in the night's probable span for him.

From what he saw and overheard, Simon Templar decided that the picture that had been drawn for him was not exaggerated, and he paid for his noxious coffee and folded his magazine and went out. The entire excursion would hardly have been worth mentioning in this anecdote at all, if it had not been for the totally unexpected complication which it unluckily led to.

The Saint had only walked a block or so along the Boulevard Clichy, and caught the attention of a prowling taxi, and discussed his destination with the chauffeur according to the protocol established by modern Paris taxi drivers (who must first be assured that the travel plans of a potential passenger fit in with their own, which they almost never do, which calls for a special bonus above the metered fare to be agreed on to compensate the driver for the inconvenience) when there was a nudge at his elbow and he turned, with a standard formula of polite but firm rebuff ready on the tip of his tongue. But instead of the painted or the pandering nonentity that he expected, he looked into a mournful emaciated-spaniel face that he knew only too well, for it belonged to Inspector Archimède Quercy of the *Police Judiciaire*.

"You will permit me to ride with you?" said the Inspector, making the question mark barely perceptible. "The George Cinq is not far out of my way, and it would be agreeable to rest my feet."

"But of course," said the Saint, with a delighted geniality which he did not feel. "After all the jokes I've made about that occupational malady of policemen, it's about time I did something to alleviate it."

In the cab, he closed the glass partition that separated them from the driver.

"And which of the nude spectacles have you been checking on?" he continued quizzically. "I had no idea it was one of the duties of the *Police Judiciaire* to go around making surprise examinations of show girls' costumes, to catch anyone trying to chisel a millimetre off the legal minimum of eight centimetres tapering to four."

"And I," said Quercy, with the utmost composure, "had no idea that the Saint was interested in such canaille as Pierrot-le-Fût."

Simon's bantering gaze did not waver, in spite of the leaden feeling that sagged within him as his premonition was so bluntly confirmed.

"Then how did you acquire this extraordinary notion?"

"Purely by observation. I give you my word, I have not been having you watched. By accident, I happened to see you in a café as I passed. I was about to cross the street to speak to you, when I noticed that in certain small ways you were not comporting yourself as I am used to seeing you. These were not things that would have caught the eye of anyone else—indeed, they were things that would help you to escape attention. It was clear, then, that you did not *want* to be seen."

"Which naturally made you want to see."

"It is a professional instinct," said the other calmly. "You soon left this first café and went to another, which was equally unlike the kind of place where one is accustomed to find the elegant Simon Templar. But again, you were trying not to appear elegant. And since you did not trail anyone there, it became evident that you were looking for someone. This was substantiated when, after a while, you walked to the third *bistro,* again not following anyone, again trying to efface yourself, and again devoting yourself to a magazine which I had already seen you read twice."

"It's a pity it was so absorbing, or I might have felt you breathing down my neck."

"Obviously it had not occurred to you that anyone might be following you : therefore you must believe that in this affair, whatever it is, you have all the initiative."

"Did Emile Gaboriau get any of his inspiration from you?"

"He could have, but I was not so old then . . . *Eh bien*, at last you discover Pierrot-le-Fût. He does not recognize you, and you are not wearing a false beard, so one deduces easily that he is not aware of your interest in him. But although you hardly exist for anyone else, you can be so skilful at submerging yourself on the rare occasions when you choose to, it is *you* I am watching from my concealment outside. I suspect you identify him from a picture or a description that has been given you, since it is manifest that you have never met, and the identification is ratified for you when his friends call him Pierrot. I see you studying him closely from behind your magazine, for a long time, until you seem to be satisfied and you leave."

"And what makes you think I was looking for this Pierrot character, out of all the others I must have looked at while you were spying on me?"

"You did not look at any others in the same way. And after you had finished studying him, you left, and you did not try any more bars. You hailed this taxi and asked to be taken to your hotel. When I heard that, I knew that you had accomplished your object, at least for the present, and I allowed myself to intrude on you."

Simon threw back his head and laughed almost inaudibly.

"If you don't qualify for some sort of award, I'll have to institute one for you," he said. "What would you think of calling it the *Prix Poulet*? . . . Now, let me tell you. I've had such a bellyful of some of these elegant places where one is accustomed to find me, as you put it, that I had an overwhelming urge tonight to go slumming. I wanted to sit in some dull dives and look at some drab characters of the type that I sometimes ran into in the bad old days.

Obviously I had to try to make myself inconspicuous, or at least not too much like an American tourist. But things don't seem the same as they used to seem. Or maybe it's me who is getting old. But I sat in a couple of joints without finding anything to be nostalgic about, and then in the last one there was this Pierrot, a survival from what seems like another era. I watched him for a while, and concluded that he was no longer amusing, only a gross bullying pig. I decided to stop trying to recapture the past and return to the soporific civilization of the Champs-Elysées."

Quercy nodded sympathetically.

"I understand you perfectly," he said. "And therefore I have to warn you that although Pierrot-le-Fût is without doubt a pig of outstanding swinishness, the responsibility for slaughtering him must be left to a French court and the authorized machinery of the State."

"When do you think they will get around to it?"

"That is not for me to predict, Monsieur Templar. But after this, if anything violent should happen to Pierre Norval that cannot instantly be attributed to his equally abominable associates, I predict that I shall be obliged to investigate every possibility that it was an act of the Saint."

"Do you mean," asked the Saint incredulously, "that you don't believe me?"

The Inspector rubbed his sad sunken jowls forbearingly.

"We have been through more than one case together, and I have learned a great respect and fondness for you, *mon cher ami*. But I do not forget the record which was the first thing I had to study about you, and I do not think you have quite overcome all your bad habits—especially when you mock a serious *policier*."

They had arrived at the hotel. Simon got out, and said with unabated impudence: "Must we make it such an early night? How about bringing your tape measure and we'll walk over and process the G-strings at the Crazy Horse Saloon?"

But Quercy shook his head and remained in the cab. *"Merci.* I am too comfortable now, so I shall ride the rest of the way home. But I beg you, do not forget what I have said. For I shall not forget."

"Everyone should have his beautiful memories, Archimède," said the Saint.

But upstairs in his suite, he paced the floor for half an hour before he could relax enough even to lie down on the bed.

The wild coincidence that Quercy had chanced to spot him in the first café, and had deployed such unexpected talents for analytical observation, had transformed with one malign stroke what should have been a virtually kindergarten exercise in meritorious homicide into a disconcertingly serious hazard.

The Saint was even less inclined to allow Pierrot-le-Fût to continue to pollute the universe than he had been when he set out for Montmartre that night; but he had no intention of losing his head over the project, figuratively or literally—and Inspector Quercy had made the latter possibility much too explicit for complacency.

The mopping-up of Pierre Norval would have to be as clean a job as the Saint had ever engineered.

It was not until he was horizontal, but still tussling frustratedly with the problem, that he had a sudden dazzling recollection of a certain cocktail party and the pompously infuriating Dr. Wilmot Javers.

There was a BEA flight to London at eleven o'clock in the morning which he was able to catch with no indecent scrambling, and thanks to the anomaly of daylight-saving time he arrived in England a little earlier than he had left France. He called Dr. Javers from the first telephone he could reach at the airport, and was fortunate to catch him at his office.

"You remember, you warned me your puzzle would haunt me," he said, with shamelessly hypocritical humility. "I didn't believe you at the time, but eventually it did. But I simply don't have the technical knowledge to solve it. Anyway, this being the first time I've been back here since you gave me that headache, the top-priority item on my list is to get you to put me out of my misery."

He could hear the man's jocund gurgle of self-satisfaction.

"I remember our little talk perfectly. And I think you've suffered enough. Can you dine with me tonight at my club? It just happens to be the evening I keep free for my scientific reading, but for an occasion like this the *Medical Journal* can wait!"

Dr. Javers was just as unctuously patronizing when they met, and maliciously refused to be the first to bring up the reason for their meeting. Simon outwaited him through two Dry Sacks and a lot of small talk, and finally had the minor satisfaction of forcing the other to advert to the topic after they had sat down to dinner.

"So you couldn't stand it any longer, eh? You admit that was one mystery that stumped you?"

"You can have it in writing if you like. But don't make me rack my feeble brain any longer."

Dr. Javers took his time, sipping a spoonful of soup and savouring it deliberately along with his moment of triumph.

"The subject was poisoned by carbon tetrachloride—otherwise, the commonest kind of cleaning fluid."

Simon stared at him, blinking.

"I thought that was supposed to be harmless. Unless he drank it. But I'm positive you never gave me any hint that he might have done that."

"I didn't, and he didn't. The clue I gave you was the lipstick stain on his coat. Although it was comparatively innocent, he probably thought it would be better to get rid of it than have to explain it to his wife. He got out a bottle of this cleaner and started to work on it. But, being in the condition he was, he knocked the bottle over and spilt what there was in it. After that, he gave up and went to bed."

"But if a few fumes like that can kill someone, from something that everybody uses, why aren't people dropping dead all the time?"

"It's a wonder it doesn't happen more often. Everyone thinks carbon tet is harmless, but that's because it doesn't catch fire or explode. The fumes are quite poisonous—a concentration of five thousand parts per million, with an exposure of only five minutes, can cause damage that may be fatal after a week's illness. That is, about a quart of fluid vaporized in a small space like the dressing room where the subject slept."

"Do you mean he was using a whole quart bottle of cleaning fluid?"

"Certainly not. But neither was he exposed for only five minutes. That's why the average user gets away with it—even if they're leaning over the thing they're cleaning and inhaling lots of fumes, they don't do it for long. The subject slept in this small room for more than four hours. In that length of time, a few ounces could have fatal results. And on top of this, there was one other factor which I was careful to emphasize."

Simon figured that he had eaten his humble pie, so he was no longer obligated to play guessing games.

"Which was that?"

"Now, really, I should have thought any detective would have spotted that one. I refer to the fact that the subject had been drinking heavily. For some reason which is not yet fully understood, alcohol sharply reduces the ability of the liver and kidneys to detoxify carbon tetrachloride. So that for a person who is under the influence, the probably lethal dose can be cut by about thirty per cent. Put these factors together, and you can calculate that it didn't take any extraordinary amount of fluid to kill the subject I told you about, in the circumstances I described."

The Saint thoughtfully finished his soup, enjoying it every bit as much as the doctor had enjoyed his, and considered various angles while the traditionally venerable club waiter was replacing it with a plate of delicately browned *sole meunière*.

Then he said: "Perhaps it's just as well more people don't know all that, or there might be a whole rash of mysterious murders."

"Don't you believe it," Javers said scornfully. "Carbon tet evaporates, yes, but it isn't undetectable. Any good pathologist would recognize the effects at once, from the way it dissolves the fat in the body organs—just as it dissolves grease spots from your clothes. So any murderer who was planning to use it would have to be damn sure it could be taken for an accident. And that's the problem with practically any other poison, as you must know."

Simon nodded respectfully. He could see no flaw that would be a handicap to him.

He knew that his subject slept in a small room and went to bed well marinated in alcohol every night; and he could safely assume that Pierrot-le-Fût slept with the shutters tightly closed, like the average Frenchman of his class, in defence against the deleterious miasmas of the night. He also knew the hours during which Yvonne Norval would be scouring and vacuuming the corridors of the George V, consolidating any alibi she might ever need.

Dr. Wilmot Javers, flicking bright gloating glances at him between dissecting operations on his sole, thought he could read the Saint's mind like a book.

"Of course, *you* might have been able to get away with it, for one of those so-called 'justice' killings they say you did in your young days, where there was no obvious motive to connect you with the victim. It's too bad you couldn't think of it for yourself then. It's too late now, because if I read in the paper about anything that sounded as if you'd made use of it, I'd feel morally bound to go to the police and tell them how I might have given you the idea. I don't approve of people taking the law into their own hands."

Simon Templar was able to smile beatifically. Fate, true to its kindly form, had finally paid its indemnity for the time and irritation that this odious coxcomb had cost him.

To make one more flying visit to Paris under another name, avoiding all places in the category of the George V, and wearing some simple disguise that this time would obviate the risk of accidental recognition by Archimède Quercy or any of his ilk, would present no great difficulty to the Saint. And he felt reasonably confident that the unspectacular demise of a low-echelon Parisian hood like Pierrot-le-Fût would not rate any space in the English press.

"Good heavens, chum," he protested. "Everyone knows I gave that up years ago."

SIMON TEMPLAR watched with a remorselessly calculating eye the quantity of caviar that was being spooned on to his plate, with the eternal springing hope that this would intimidate the head waiter into serving a more than normally generous portion, and said: "If I had to answer such a silly question as why I want to be rich, I'd say it was so I could afford to eat those unhatched sturgeon twice a day. There must be some moral in the thought that they're considered the national delicacy of Russia, the self-styled protector of the under-privileged."

He waved away the tray of minced onion and chopped whites and yolks of eggs proffered by a lesser servitor, and signalled the wine steward who waited near by with a frosted bottle.

"Romanoff caviar and Romanoff vodka—what a wonderful proletarian combination!"

"I always did like your ideas of the simple life," said Monty Hayward comfortably.

The Saint piled a small mound of black grains on a thin slice of brown toast, tasted it reverently, and raised his glass.

"I read somewhere that the scientists have discovered a rare vitamin in caviar which greatly increases the human system's ability to stand up to alcohol—I'm not kidding," he remarked. "I suppose the Russians, who always claim to have discovered everything, would say that they knew this all along. That's why they put away so much of this stuff at their banquets. Well, don't quote me to the FBI, but I prefer this to the American excuse for vodka-tippling."

"And what's that?" Monty asked unguardedly.

"The sales pitch that it doesn't change the flavour of whatever slop you dilute it with; and that it doesn't taint your breath—so that if you wreck a few cars on the way home, and you can still stand up, the cops presumably won't dream you've been drinking. This may be predicated on the erroneous assumption that cops can't read advertisements, too, but I suppose it gives some people confidence. I shall let you drive us home, Monty. *Na zdorovye*!"

"Here's to crime," Monty said.

Simon regarded him affectionately.

They were dining at the East Arms at Hurley, a one-time English country pub which was its own sufficient answer to some of the old traditional gibes at British gastronomical facilities, and it was their first reunion in many years. It was a very far cry from the days when Monty Hayward had sometimes found himself involved in the fringes of the Saint's lawless activities, and in particular had been embroiled in one incredible adventure which had whirled them across Austria and Bavaria in a fantastic flight that may still be remembered by senior students of these chronicles.

"It's been a long time, Monty," said the Saint. "And now you're a Director of the Consolidated Press, with an expense account and a chauffeured limousine and all the trimmings, and you wouldn't get mixed up in any of my chenanigans for anything. Don't you ever get tired of this awful respectability?"

"Never," declared Monty firmly. "It's too nice to be able to look a policeman in the eye."

"I never saw one with such beautiful eyes, myself," said the Saint.

"I ran into another reformed friend of yours the other day, incidentally. I'd been to Cambridge with the Chairman about one of our scholarship projects, and on the way back in the evening we felt thirsty. We were going through a little village called Listend, which you won't even find on most maps, but it's just off the main road not far from Hertford, and we spotted a very quaint pub called the Golden Stag, so we stopped there. And who do you think was standing there behind the bar?"

"I'll try one guess. Gypsy Rose Lee."

"Sam Outrell—the fellow you had for a janitor when you lived at Cornwall House."

The Saint's face lighted up.

"Good old Sam! I've often wondered what happened to him."

"Well, he always said he was a country boy, you remember; and I suppose all those years of tipping you off when Inspector Teal was waiting in the lobby to see you, and inventing alibis for you when you weren't there, must have convinced him that the city life was too strenuous for the likes of him. So after he'd earned his pension, he took his savings and bought this pub."

"That's wonderful. How's he doing?"

"Not too well, right now . . . He's run into a bit of trouble."

Some of the blue in the Saint's gaze seemed to gently change latitude, from Mediterranean to arctic.

"Has he? What kind?"

"He was caught selling drinks after hours—*and* to a minor, what's more. It looks pretty bad."

"What ever made him do a stupid thing like that? I mean, getting caught."

"He swears he didn't do it, it was a frame-up. But he doesn't think he's got a chance of beating it. He's expecting to lose his licence."

"This is something that could only happen in Merrie England," said the Saint sulfurously. "I love this country; but the equating of morality with the precise hour at which somebody wants a drink is one refinement where they lost me. I am so depraved that I still admire the good sense of all those barbarous countries which cling to the primitive notion that a citizen should be entitled to a drink any time he can pay for it."

"Even a minor?"

"The kids take a glass of wine with the family in France, or beer in Germany, and I've never noticed that it seemed to do them any harm. Personally, I'd say it was a lot better for them than the soda-pop-slop they swill by the gallon in America, and that's already infiltrated here."

"Well, the chap that Sam swears he was shopped by wouldn't agree with you," Monty said. "Particularly since he's apparently got an interest in one of those soda-pop-slop factories, as you call 'em."

"This may ruin a beautiful dinner," Simon said grimly. "And the chicken pie here, which I ordered for us, is merely the best in England. But at the risk of acute indigestion, I must hear more about this ineffable excrescence."

"His name," Monty said reluctantly, "is Isaiah Thoat."

"I can hardly believe it," said the Saint, rubbing his hands together ecstatically. "But do go on."

If Mr. Isaiah Thoat's ears had begun to burn at this juncture, they would actually have added little luminosity to his complexion, in spite of their impressive size, for his facial capillaries had already endowed him with the rosy colouration which is popularly believed to be engendered by over-indulgence in ferments and distillates. It was an incongruous tint for his mournful cast of countenance, and attained its zenith of infelicity at the end of his long nose, which was positively purple. The combination, with his unfortunately rheumy eyes and the sombre clothes which he preferred, made him look like a bibulous undertaker. This was a cruel injustice, for he had never tasted anything even as potent as lager beer, and the only burial he aspired to supervise was that of the allegorical figure personified as John Barleycorn.

Even Mr. Thoat's bitterest opponents, who were legion, had never found grounds for questioning his sincerity. But it could be claimed with equal truth that the Emperor Nero, the directors of the Spanish Inquisition, and the hierarchy of the Nazi Party were also sincere, according to their lights. And Isaiah Thoat would not have had to take second place to any of them for the fanaticism with which he was prepared to persecute dissenters from his dogma that liquor was the root of all evil.

"There he stood, Mr. Templar," said Sam Outrell, "right where you are, an' no witnesses, of course, an' sez: 'Between you an' me, I'd borrow the devil's own pitchfork if I could use it to help toss some of you traders in Satan's poison into his own Hades'."

"And he used his own daughter to coax a drink out of you?" Simon asked.

"As true as I'm standin' here, so help me. I wouldn't have no cause to lie to you, sir, you know that, much as I've done it *for* you in the old days. She's just as 'omely as he is, what you'd expect, with that breeding, an' it makes her look a lot older. But I didn't have the foggiest who she was, an' I fell for the whole swindle like a ton o' bricks."

"What did she do?"

"It's closing time, an' she's about the last customer left, an' she sez she feels faint. Now, she ain't had nothing to account for that, I know, 'cause I served her meself all evening, an' all she drank was that Sanitade stuff her father makes—though I didn't know then he was her father. So I gets everybody else out, while the wife is fussin' over her, an' this young woman sez 'Could I have a sip of brandy?' "

"She asked for it herself?"

"Oh, yes—very weak like, as if she might die any minute. Well, sir, what would *you* do?"

Simon nodded in anticipation.

"And as soon as you gave it to her, the door opens——"

"Which I'd bin too bothered to lock up, an' there's a bobby comin' in. 'I seen you through the window,' he sez, 'selling this girl a drink.'

" 'She's a friend of ours an' a guest in the house,' I sez, knowin' the Law. 'We didn't sell her nothing, we gave it to her.'

"Right away she ain't faintin' no more, but sittin' up as fine as you please, an' she sez 'That's a lie,' she sez, 'I bought and paid for it.' An' there she's pointin' to a half-crown on the bar which she must've put down while we were talkin'. I ask you, sir, what chance did I have?"

The Saint took a sympathetically thoughtful swig from his tankard.

"Did you tell all this to the Beak?"

"Of course I did. An' he sez he has a mind to send me to jail for perjury. Because this girl, which ain't what I'd like to call her, is there in court with her father, Mr. Thoat, an' he backs her up."

"They were in it together?"

"It looks like it. 'She's a wayward girl and a cross I have to bear, your Honour,' he sez. 'In spite of all I've done, this craving for the devil's brew comes over her. That's why I asked the constable to keep an eye out for her. It only takes an opportunity like this despicable publican gave her,' he sez, 'to undo all my loving care. I ask your Honour to make an example of him.' "

"And he did?"

"This magistrate is a teetotaller himself, an' a real holy terror. He fines me a hundred quid, an' sez he'll consider havin' my licence taken away. I don't think I've got an earthly, Mr. Templar."

Outrell looked around the low-ceilinged room with its age-blackened beams and yellowed plaster, the honestly worn chairs and tables of uncertain vintage, the bare floor eroded in ancient contours compounded of the vagaries of its own wood grain and the most-used routes between bar and bench and dart-board, all exposed in their nakedest simplicity by the bright morning light that streamed through the leaded windows; and his big hands tightened into stolid pain-enduring fists. It was just after opening time, and there were no other customers to listen or interrupt.

"This is all I ever wanted, sir. Even when I went to work in London, to earn more money for bringing up the kids than I could as a farm hand. A place like this to put what was left of our savings in, where the wife an' me could make enough to get along without being a burden to anyone includin' the other taxpayers, an' we could have good company every day, with the kind o' plain country people we like. Thank God the old English country pub is still goin' strong, Mr. Templar, in spite of Mr. Thoat an' his Sanitade. It's as English as the changin' of the Guard, or the Derby, or them orators in Hyde Park : it's the little man's club an' debating society an' a place to get away from the missus when she's actin' up without gettin' into no real trouble, where he can have his mug o' beer an' good company an' not get hurt or hurt nobody. I thought I could be a good publican, though he sez it as if it was a rude word——It hurts, Mr. Templar, but p'raps after all I wasn't cut out for it. It hurts; but me an' the wife are readin' the advertisements, lookin' for something else. We might have to take a little tobacco an' sweet shop, something like that, somewhere. But it won't be the same."

"Have you any idea why they picked on you?"

"I suppose that's not hard to see, if you make yourself think like he does. His Sanitade company bought all the land next to me, from here to the main road, for their new Garden Factory. You must've noticed the foundations goin' in when you drove up. That's it. He thinks it'd be terrible to have a common pub right next to the plant where his Angels of Abstinence Association are mixin' up their swill—not to mention the danger to his precious workers who might be tempted to drop in here for a quick one at lunch time or on the way home. He tried to get me to sell, when I moved in here, that time I started off tellin' you about; an' when I said I was goin' to stay, an' couldn't we live an' let live, that's when he swore he'd get me out whatever it took. But what's the use o' tellin' that to a magistrate, especially one like that one? He's against you from the start, an' anything you say is just tryin' to wriggle out of a conviction. I know when I ain't got a chance."

"You're putting me in the hell of a spot, Sam," said the Saint. "All these years I've had a dim hope that Prohibition might really take over in England, and then we could all become bootleggers and get rich. But if this front man for the Cause has to be mowed down, for your sake, I'll see what can be done. Don't give up yet."

He went back to London to make some inquiries of his

own, of which the most delicate concerned the constable who had played an essential part in the conviction of Sam Outrell. Obtaining the police records of policemen is about as ticklish an assignment as any outsider can undertake, especially when he is as traditionally *non grata* in police circles as the Saint, and when it might later become vital that nobody should recall that he had been inquiring about the officer in question.

There is however a section in the War Office which can request such information without having to give reasons, and which at certain periods has gratefully accepted the services of even more irregular characters than the Saint. There was a grey colonel still there who had not forgotten an obligation incurred during the days of the Swastika, who called the Saint back very promptly and without any fuss.

"There doesn't seem to be anything wrong with him except that he may be a bit too ambitious. He put in for the Scotland Yard training school, but he failed the written examination and went back to the Hertford constabulary. He's entered for another try next year. They give him good marks locally except for taking himself too seriously and trying to get ahead too fast."

The supplementary data on Isaiah Thoat were much easier to get, being mostly matters of public record. A former lay preacher, food faddist, pacifist, and antivivisectionist, he had finally settled on *spiritus frumenti* as the ideal lifelong adversary, and in that cause had formed and dedicated and made himself President of the Angels of Abstinence Association. But unlike the creators of many similar organizations, Mr. Thoat had a hard head as well as a chip on his shoulder, and he had learned from other efforts to divert the human race from doom and damnation that Mammon is a powerful ally in righteous as well as unrighteous persuasion, and that the Righteous are often uncomfortably short of this assistance. Therefore he had arranged for the subscriptions, donations, and other funds picked up by the Angels of Abstinence to be funnelled into the manufacture and marketing of a potion that they could all themselves enjoy without fear of divine or digestive retribution, which they could personally propagandize wherever they went with the comforting assurance that no souls would be even superficially scorched, but that the coffers of salvation would be enriched by every sip.

Thus was born Sanitade, a nectar loosely based on a chocolated broth which Mr. Thoat's mother had made for him when he broke out in teenage pimples, fortified with fruit juices chosen for their vitamin content, this horrendous concoction being well pasteurized, carbonated, and sealed in non-returnable bottles. The cachet of manufacture by the Angels of Abstinence gave it the same sort of distinction as is enjoyed, in the opposing camp, by the liqueur brewed by the Benedictine monks, and practically forced its acceptance and indorsement by all other groups dedicated to the same tenets as the Angels even under different management. It had thus become almost the official potion of all dry crusaders, and from them had spread to the membership of many equally zealous if less monophobic organizations, until Mr. Thoat could congratulate himself on having been rewarded with quite a thriving business for his battle against those other beverages which he maintained, also fuelled the fires of Hell, causing them to burn with a blue flame.

"We must do something about him, Monty," Simon Templar said at another encounter.

"Why?" Monty argued. "Live and let live. Let him

enjoy preaching prohibition and let us enjoy our drinks, then everybody's happy."

"Except Sam."

"He might do better selling cigarettes and gum drops, after all. The country-pub business isn't what it used to be when you and I were a bit younger, anyway. And if you want to start that Robin Hood stuff again, you should do it on something important. There are still people smuggling dope into this country, for instance. It was in the papers only yesterday that Scotland Yard is baffled——"

"Maybe I'll help them with that, too," said the Saint. "As soon as I can spare the time. But, Monty, have you ever tasted Sanitade?"

"No; and I don't want to. I have a rather sensitive stomach——"

"I understand that. It *looks* sensitive, since you became an Editorial Director. So you should have more sympathy for other people who are being afflicted. It's almost a sacred duty to get that swill off the market. And if we can strike a blow against crackpots and help Sam at the same time, wouldn't it make you feel young again?"

The old hypnotic devilment danced in the Saint's blue eyes, and Monty Hayward groaned.

"It makes me wish I'd had the sense to keep my mouth shut," he said.

No such rueful presentiment clouded the horizon of Mr. Isaiah Thoat as he watched the first rather unceremonious activation of the Sanitade Garden Plant—that would be a better name than "Factory," he was thinking, and fitted the "Garden" motif so nicely.

The activation in fact consisted only of the delivery of a truck-load of cacao to an old but well-built barn which had been the only edifice on the plant site when he acquired it, which he had thriftily decided to preserve and use for miscellaneous storage. Though the new buildings were barely starting to rise from their footings, his shrewdness was already being vindicated : he had had the chance to pick up this consignment of essential raw material at a giveaway price, but would have had to turn it down if he had been limited to the storage facilities of the outgrown original Sanitade Factory which he was preparing to replace.

"You see, my dear Selina," he observed to his daughter, who was with him, "Fortune does not only aid the wicked. Good luck is usually the reward of good judgement."

"And you deserve all that you get, Papa," she said.

She was one of those unlucky young females who seem to have been created solely to boost the morale of their nearest competitors. Beside her, no other creature in a skirt could have felt hopeless. It might be kinder not to detail her specifications, but simply to say that for every apparently ultimate disaster in feminine architecture there must be something worse; and she was it.

Mr. Thoat signed the driver's receipt and himself closed and locked the barn doors. He was just completing this when County Constable George Yelland rode by on his bicycle, and stopped.

"Good morning, sir—and Miss Selina," said the young man, saluting smartly. "I see that you're moving in already, in quite a big way."

"Good morning, officer," said Mr. Thoat agreeably. "But what gave you the idea——"

"A large lorry has just stopped here, sir," said the constable airily. "The tracks are quite plain, where it pulled in, and considerably lighter where it pulled out. Therefore, it discharged quite a load. It rained this morning from 5:10 A.M. until 7:35. The tracks were made since the rain, and since I find you here locking the door I conclude that the delivery has just taken place."

"Excellent," said Mr. Thoat. "I only wish that some of those vulgar popular writers who seem to take such a delight in deriding the British police could be forced to observe you on your rounds. I shall write another letter to the Chief Constable about you—you *are* the young officer who took such good care of my daughter recently, aren't you?"

He had not noticed that his offspring had returned the constable's greeting with the swooning adoration of a dyspeptic sheep.

"Yes, Mr. Thoat, I had that privilege——But what I'm concerned about now is whether it's wise for you to leave anything valuable in this barn. I've noticed the contractor doesn't keep a night watchman here."

"I declined to underwrite that expense," Mr. Thoat said primly. "It's up to him to see that there aren't so many materials left lying around that it's worth some professional loafer's wages just to protect them from petty pilfering."

"Yes, sir; but building jobs do catch the eye of a certain type of petty thief, and then a building like this barn becomes a sort of attraction, out here in the middle of nowhere, so to speak, where nobody would be likely to hear anyone breaking in."

"Then I shall rely on you to keep an especially sharp watch on it, Constable——"

"Yelland, sir."

"Ah, yes. I must remember that name, so that your services will be properly credited by the authorities if my property is protected—or vice versa. I'm sure we are leaving everything in good hands—are we not, Selina?"

"Yes, indeed, Papa," said Selina, with more than dutiful ardour.

Mr. Thoat consulted his watch.

"I must be going, or I shall be late for my appointment in town. That wretched plumber should have been here an hour ago. Now he'll just have to come back another time."

"I could wait for him, Papa, and go back on the bus. I can tell him what you decided about the wash-rooms."

"An excellent idea. And be sure he understands that I refuse to pay extra for such frivolities as coloured tiles."

Mr. Thoat drove himself back to London—he had a nine-year-old car which he never propelled beyond twenty miles an hour, thereby having caused several accidents to happen to other drivers who had been goaded to recklessness by the sheer exasperation of dragging behind him. But he had allowed plenty of time for his customary average, and arrived at the modest South Kensington teashoppe where he had made his luncheon rendezvous a few minutes before his guest, who had dallied until the last moment at the nearest tavern, taking prophylaxis against the aridity of the impending meal.

"I'm sorry to have kept you waiting, Mr. Thoat."

"Not at all, Mr. Tombs, I was early," Mr. Thoat said generously.

He took out his wallet, extracted from it a neatly written cheque, and passed it across the table.

Simon Templar took it, verified the amounts, and put it away in his own billfold with equal gravity. He was wearing an old-fashioned double-breasted suit and tie of almost canonical drabness, and only the most assiduous students of his techniques of disguise would have recognized him. With a heavy powdering of white in the hair, the roughed-up eyebrows, and the untidy false moustache,

behind an eye-shield of tinted glasses, and bowed in a
concave-chested slouch, there was little to recall the
dynamic exuberance that he wore like a halo when he
chose to live up to more appropriate names than Tombs.

"The delivery was all right, then, was it, Mr. Thoat?"

"Oh, yes, Mr. Tombs. Perfectly correct. I hope you
aren't offended by my reserving payment until it was
completed; but after all, in making such a purchase from
a total stranger, at so much below the current market
price——"

"Don't think any more about it, Mr. Thoat. I understand. Of course I'm losing money. But I'm helping a good
cause. And I can take the loss off my income tax. That
makes it about the same as a donation, doesn't it?"

"Yes, certainly, but——"

"But I can't go on selling to you at a loss, Mr. Thoat.
I'm supposed to make my living in the commodity market.
The Government would begin to get suspicious. I have
been looking for another approach."

"Do you gennelmun wanta order?" inquired an impatient waitress, leaning over with a threatening notebook.

The menu offered the grisly alternatives of boiled
sausages, fricassée of veal, or a Health Salad compounded
of raw vegetables, fruits, and nuts. It was obvious which
of these delicacies Mr. Thoat would order. Simon settled
for the boiled sausages, steeling himself against Mr.
Thoat's slightly pained expression with a placating bottle
of Sanitade, and hoped that he would be able to get it
down without a visible shudder.

"I'm not a capitalist, Mr. Thoat—the income tax
system has seen to that," he resumed. "But I do receive
the income from a trust fund set up by my late father,
which I don't really need. Since he accumulated this
money by putting aside and investing each year the

amount which he estimated he would have spent on drink if he had been a drinker, I think he would approve of my passing it on to help you in your wonderful work."

"It would certainly be well employed," said Mr. Thoat, a trifle shakily. "And I'm flattered that you should have chosen me, out of all the possible——"

"That was not flattery, or a random selection, Mr. Thoat. Frankly, I have investigated several deserving organizations of the same type as yours. What impressed me, as a business man, about the Angels of Abstinence, is that they are run on a practical businesslike basis which actively aids and in no way compromises their idealistic objectives. I understand that you alone are responsible for this. That makes you the man for me. To get the most out of the income I am talking about calls for a business man as well as a crusader. It amounts to about sixteen thousand pounds a year."

Mr. Thoat somehow managed not to choke on the first mouthful of shredded fodder which had just been set before him.

"I think I shall be able to justify your confidence, Mr. Tombs."

"There are, of course, a few conditions."

"Of what kind?"

"Purely technical, in your case; but I feel I must pass them on to you, since they're the same as the ones which the trust imposes on me. What they amount to is that your life must be absolutely blameless, even above suspicion. That you must never be convicted of an offence against public decorum, of riotous behaviour, scandalous conduct, criminal associations, drunkenness or even having taken a drink—all that sort of thing. It's all in the deed which I've told my lawyer to draw up."

"I hardly think that will be any problem," said Mr. Thoat, with a certain indulgent smugness.

"I'm sure it won't—but in the fantastic event that any such thing should occur, all payments would automatically stop, or never start. We have to take that precaution, the lawyers tell me. Then you will have to give a few simple undertakings on how the money will *not* be spent— such as advertising in periodicals which also accept liquor advertising, you know the sort of thing——"

They talked of this and kindred matters for the rest of the meal—if that word can be applied to the ingestion of such provender as they had been served.

"I hope we can meet and sign this deed the day after tomorrow," Simon said finally.

"The day after tomorrow?" Mr. Thoat's eyebrows went up remonstratively. "But that's Sunday!"

"I know. But I had enough trouble getting my lawyer to work tomorrow to get it done. And I hardly think that signing a couple of papers like these would be called working on the Lord's Day. Unfortunately I have to be in New York on business the first thing Monday morning— I'm taking a plane at midnight Sunday. I'd like to have this done before I leave. Just in case of accidents, you know."

Mr. Thoat nodded. The prospect of Mr. Sebastian Tombs being jet-propelled to his eternal rest by some mechanical malfunction in mid-Atlantic, with this munificent endowment uncompleted, gave him a cold shiver.

"I understand. But as I think I've mentioned, this Sunday is rather a busy day for me."

Simon knew that, too. There was about to break out in London another of those international conventions with which every major city must periodically be afflicted; only this was not the type which has consolations for saloon-keepers, night club impresarios, and ladies of flexible morality, like the average run of these jamborees, being billed as a World Temperance Congress of groups whose avowed objective was the ruin of all such iniquitous entrepreneurs. It was to be launched that Sunday by a grand parade of delegates from Hyde Park to Trafalgar Square, intended to dramatize the fact of their presence in town and to draw expectant attention to the week of speechmaking and resolution-adopting which was to follow, during which some of the world's most talented firebrands would denounce assorted forms of fun with all the hyperbolic savagery and violence to be expected of proper advocates of temperance.

"The parade is supposed to start at two-thirty, isn't it?" said the Saint. "I know that nothing would stop you leading the Angels of Abstinence yourself; but surely you could get away for lunch? My apartment is just off Park Lane, only two minutes from the park. If you could be there at one. I'll have a nice salad waiting, and promise to get you back with ten minutes to spare."

Mr. Thoat pursed his lips.

"Yes, I suppose I could manage that. It seems to be the only way."

"Splendid! I'll have the papers and everything ready. Now I must run—I have another appointment which just won't wait."

This was literally true, the appointment being dictated by the still unrevised licensing laws of England, which in a few minutes would ruthlessly compel the pub around the corner to close for the afternoon, thus making it impossible to satisfactorily wash away the taste of the boiled sausages and Sanitade which Simon Templar had been unable to finish. But he left Mr. Thoat in an obliviously happy daze through which even the fact that the bill for their deplorable repast still remained to be paid did not penetrate until too late.

Mr. Thoat had already relegated the transaction through which the beneficent Sebastian Tombs had introduced himself to the category of past business; but it was not so easily filed away by County Constable George Yelland, who had lingered on at the barn after Mr. Thoat took his sedate departure.

"What exactly are you keeping here?" asked the earnest young officer.

"Cocoa beans," said Selina Thoat airily.

"Oh. I suppose they're not really too valuable to leave here."

"Not unless somebody stole all of them. That would come to quite a lot. Papa got these at a bargain. Are you married?"

Constable Yelland managed not to jump.

"No, miss."

"There's a dance in Hertford tomorrow night. I wish I could go."

"I hadn't heard about it."

"I wish you could take me."

"I don't think your father would approve of that, miss."

"Papa will be busy in London, with a welcoming dinner for some of our people. But he could do a lot for you— putting in a word about you in the right places—if I asked him to."

"Thank you, miss. But I'm afraid I'm on duty Saturday night. It's always a busy time."

"I could help you, too. Like I did that night at the Golden Stag."

Constable Yelland tried to ignore a sensation of extraordinary discomfort.

"I hope you didn't do anything beyond your duty to

tell the truth, miss. Now if you'll excuse me, I've got a lot of miles to cover on this round——"

She watched him thoughtfully as he mounted his bicycle and pedalled away.

George Yelland, however, as an aspirant to the higher honours of the CID, was not the kind of policeman to remove a thought from his mind, once it had entered it, as efficiently as he had been taught to remove his person from unprofessional situations. The responsibility of Mr. Thoat's barn stayed with him, accentuated by a vaguely unsatisfied query about its contents, which caused him to keep it under even closer surveillance than was called for by simple self-interest.

He made a particular point of passing by several times the next day, since the workmen were observing the union Sabbath; and it was in the afternoon that he discovered a car parked off the road where the builder's trucks had furrowed an entrance, and a man studying the barn with a kind of interest that could be definitely described as calculating.

This was no insignificant tribute to the histrionic ability of Monty Hayward, who on the Saint's instructions had been trying to maintain that effect for more than an hour before the constable arrived.

"May I ask what you're doing here?" Yelland said, as the book prescribed.

"Casing the joint," Monty said easily.

"May I have your name, sir?"

The "sir" was another sort of tribute, not so much to Monty's air of confidence as to his distinctly unburglar-like appearance. Monty produced a card which gave his address with the Consolidated Press but made no mention of his status as a director—apart from a genuine natural modesty which he did his best to conceal, it still amused him at times to play at being an ordinary reporter again, a game which those unostentatious cards made perpetually possible.

"Now that I've identified myself," Monty said amiably. "What's *your* name?"

"Yelland, sir."

"Yelland? Where have I heard that name recently? . . . Oh, yes. You're the Robert who raided the pub down the road, and caught 'em selling a drink after hours to the young daughter of the chap who's building this factory."

"It wasn't exactly a raid, sir. Mr. Thoat asked me to keep an eye on his daughter, and it's my duty to look out for violations of the law."

"Of course. But didn't you think there was something a bit fishy about that conviction?"

Constable Yelland had another of those remotely unsettling qualms which had afflicted him since the previous morning.

"That isn't for me to say, sir. I only gave evidence as to what I saw and heard with my own eyes and ears. It's the magistrate who makes the conviction."

"Oh, come off it, Robert!"

"The name is George, sir."

"All right, Robert George. You've got opinions of your own, haven't you?"

"It's against regulations for me to discuss the decision of a court in which I have been a witness, sir," said the constable, taking refuge in asperity from his own uncertainty. "And anyhow, what are you so interested about?"

Monty Hayward grinned, and brought out a pipe and tobacco-pouch which he began to work together with a disarming assurance which he had practised in some considerably more risky situations than this one.

"Suppose I was doing an article on Mr. Thoat," he said.

"I'd be interested in a lot of things. Not just that business about his daughter, though that might come into it. But about what's going on here, too. For instance, do you know what he's got in this barn?"

"Yes. Cocoa."

"Ah."

"What do you mean, Ah?"

"I only mean that items like that are what sometimes make headlines."

"I don't see what's a headline in that."

"Do you know where he got this cocoa?"

"No, sir. Only that it was a bargain."

"He told you that, did he?"

"His daughter did."

"That was careless of her."

"Look here, sir," Yelland said, with increasing impatience, "if you know something that I ought to know, it's your duty to tell me, not tease me with it."

"I don't definitely know anything," Monty replied. "Not yet. Suspicions aren't evidence, as you know. But I am investigating what sounded like a rather hot tip——"

"Where did it come from?"

Monty gave a reproachful look.

"Now, officer, you know very well that no reporter would give away the source of some kinds of information, and even a judge couldn't force him to. I can only tell you that it came from an acquaintance of mine who isn't always on good terms with the police, but who usually knows what he's talking about. I've got a few more inquiries to make here and there, and if they confirm each other there may be an interesting arrest. Would you like to make an interesting arrest?"

The spontaneous gleam in the young policeman's eye

was replaced almost instantly by a dampening recognition of fact.

"I'm not in the CID yet, sir."

"But you'd like to be, wouldn't you? You're a lot smarter than a lot of chaps on a beat, I've noticed that. I wish I *could* give you a——"

Suddenly Monty Hayward froze, staring fixedly, one hand extending with his pipe pointing in the direction of the stare.

"Robert George, do you see that?"

"What, sir?"

"That piece of paper, just sticking out from under the barn door! Go and get it. This may save us all the trouble of applying for a search warrant!"

Constable Yelland perplexedly retrieved the fragment. It appeared to be the corner of a label, but the only printing that could be read on it was the words: LATROPIC IMPORT COMPANY, CUTTS LANE, STEPNEY.

"Cocoa is a tropical product," Monty said. "I think we can assume that the label came from some of the stuff that was delivered here."

"Very likely, sir. But I still don't see——"

"Of course not. But you will . . . Hang on to the clue, officer. And let me know where you can be reached tomorrow morning, especially if you're off duty. I'll pass the tip on to you before anyone else, if it turns out to be a sound one, and you can make the most of it. Meanwhile mum's the word."

Constable Yelland found himself left in a dreamy cloud not entirely unlike the one which had befogged Mr. Thoat when Simon Templar took leave of him the day before. Which was not a fantastic coincidence, since the technique for creating both befuddlements had originated in the same disgracefully handsome head.

"A very nice job, Monty," said the Saint, when he had listened to an almost verbatim report. "I don't think you missed a trick. With a little more practice and a few less suburban scruples, you could soon be the perfect partner in crime again."

"Thanks very much," Monty said. "But I never was. This was an easy job, and it can't get me into any trouble, whatever happens. I can still hide behind the Consolidated Press and the professional secrecy excuse. But when I think what it would be like if we'd been caught breaking into that Latropic warehouse, I wonder if I was ever qualified to be a company director."

"Lots of them have ended up in jail," Simon pointed out reassuringly. "But I'd've got you out of it somehow. Didn't I always?"

"Like you did in that business about Prince Rudolf and his crown jewels. Yes; but my ageing nerves can't take so much any more. And suppose Young Sherlock identifies me as the driver of the truck that delivered that cocoa yesterday?"

The Saint laughed at him shamelessly.

"He never saw you. And Isaiah never looked at you twice—you said that yourself. And anyhow, I made you up and messed you up until even I wondered what you really looked like. And I stole the truck myself while you were in a board meeting with some of the best alibis on Fleet Street. Now will you stop worrying long enough to work out the timing for tomorrow?"

"It seems to me that our timing's a bit off already. I've been watching for a report on that Latropic robbery, and there still doesn't seem to have been one."

"Because their warehouse isn't opened every day, only when shipments are coming in or going out. We did a nice quiet job that didn't attract any attention in the neighbourhood, and obviously they didn't have any reason to go to the place on Friday. That's the first thing to take care of. You just use your reporter's immunity again, call the head man at home and say you've heard through the underworld grapevine that his storehouse was cracked, and what does he know about it? If it hasn't been discovered yet, he'll soon find out. Then you see that it gets in the Sunday papers. Then tomorrow morning . . ."

At eight o'clock the next morning, George Yelland was just starting his breakfast and his Sunday paper simultaneously when his landlady called him to the telephone.

"This is the scoop I promised you, officer," Monty Hayward said, after identifying himself. "Have you seen a newspaper yet?"

"I was just starting it, sir."

"You'll find a report that the Latropic Import Company — remember that label? — had their warehouse broken into on Thursday night and a lorry load of cocoa beans stolen, but the theft wasn't discovered till yesterday afternoon, some time after I talked to you. Item two: if you check with Scotland Yard, you'll find that they have a report of a lorry being stolen from a garage on Thursday afternoon which was found abandoned at Highgate on Friday afternoon. You might find out about its tyres, and have another look at the tracks at Thoat's barn. If you want to get credit for some fast thinking, you put that together with what Thoat's daughter told you and take it to your Inspector. You needn't bring me into it—tell him you figured it all out yourself. It should be good enough to take to any magistrate you can catch on his way to church, and get a search warrant for that barn."

"But, sir . . . Mr. Thoat—a receiver of stolen goods!" Yelland's voice almost choked on the enormity of the thought as well as its possible value to his record. "They'd laugh at me, and I wouldn't blame 'em!"

"The thieves knew just where to unload the stuff, didn't they, only a few hours after it was stolen? And there aren't so many people who could use all that cocoa. Didn't his daughter say it was a bargain? And where do you get some of the best bargains—if you don't ask any questions?"

"I know, sir, but——"

"Don't disappoint me, Robert," Monty insisted, and this time the constable was too spellbound to reprove him on the name. "I'm trying to do something for you, and all I want in return is that you'll see that the Consolidated Press gets the official news first. But if anyone goes on laughing at you, you suggest phoning the managing director of Latropic Import himself, and he'll tell you that they haven't sold or delivered that much cocoa to anyone, Mr. Thoat or anyone else, for more than a week. I'll give you his name and home address. Take this down . . ."

For Mr. Isaiah Thoat it was also destined to be a climactic day. After a chapel service at which he had been invited to read the First Lesson, a performance which always left him feeling that at least part of the mantle of some Old Testament prophet remained clinging to his shoulders, he had huddled with the captains of his Angels of Abstinence over last-minute parade arrangements until he was only able to arrive an apologetic five minutes late at the address on Grosvenor Street which Simon Templar was using for that operation.

The apartment itself actually belonged to a stalwart pillar of the House of Lords, who stayed there only when Parliament was in session, and even then retreated every week-end to his estate in the Cotswolds, and who would have been most surprised to know what unauthorized use

was being made of it. But with the sole aid of this elementary knowledge of his lordship's habits, and a certain
persuasive skill with a lock, the mythical personality of
Sebastian Tombs had been provided for the brief necessary time with a physical abode which could not possibly
be linked to Simon Templar by any thread of proof.

"Come in, come in," said the Saint heartily, brushing
off Mr. Thoat's excuses on the threshold. "I know it must
have been hard for you to get away."

"I took the liberty of bringing my daughter Selina,"
Mr. Thoat said, disclosing her as he entered.

"Delighted," said the Saint, without flinching. "She
can help with the salad. I'm all alone here— I don't
approve of making a servant work on Sunday, even for a
special occasion. But I think we can look after ourselves.
I was just experimenting with something I thought of
yesterday—a Sanitade cocktail. I know Sanitade is wonderful by itself, but people like to mix things, it makes
them feel smart and creative. Might be another sales angle
for you. Here, try it."

He poured from a silver cocktail shaker.

Mr. Thoat and Selina tasted, and tasted again.

"It's very good," Mr. Thoat said politely.

"Just some Angostura, ginger, peppermint, and a
couple of other things," said the Saint. "I'll send you the
recipe when it's perfected, and perhaps a few others. You
could put out a little booklet. There's nothing wrong
about fighting the Devil with his own weapons, is there?
And I think this mixture has quite a refreshing tang for
a hot day."

Mr. Thoat and Selina drank some more. It was a hot
day.

"Very good indeed," Mr. Thoat said.

His tone was a little less perfunctory, a little warmer.

The combination certainly seemed to do something. Although it obscured the pure flavour of Sanitade, which to him was delicious, it indeed had a zest which developed like a sort of delayed deeper echo to the first impact on the palate.

"I haven't forgotten our time limit," said the Saint. "So if your daughter *would* take over in the kitchen, we can get right down to business. Would you like to start reading the deed while I show her where everything is?"

It was an impressive document on which Simon had laboured conscientiously for some hours, loading it with all the whereases and heretofores that his sense of legal jargon could supply, and typing it on a grade of paper only slightly less heavy than the stone tablets which its verbiage deserved. After stretching to the limit the details of periodicity of payment, it proceeded, as he had warned at their luncheon, to prohibit at great length a list of highly improbable ways in which the money could not be spent, such as financing disorderly houses or lewd publications. From there it went on to enumerate the even more fanciful covenants assumed by Isaiah Thoat, who personally undertook to eschew such practices as nudism, consorting with astrologers, or dancing in a ballet, on down to receiving stolen goods or being charged with drunkenness, upon the least of which breaches the whole deal was off.

All this was gone through, clause by clause, while Mr. Thoat had two more Sanitade cocktails and Simon took another one out to the kitchen.

"I know it sounds almost insulting," Simon said unhappily. "But that's the kind of man my father was. Don't take anything for granted, was one of his principles. Even I had to sign the same thing myself."

"I am not offended," said Mr. Thoat, with an almost

benign superciliousness. "No man need be ashamed of reaffirming his principles. And with such a lot of money involved, you can't be coo tareful—I mean, too careful."

He scrawled his signature in the places provided, and handed the papers back with a grandiose flourish which almost upset his glass.

"Thish ish a great moment in my life," he announced. "The climaxsh of thirty yearsh of vedotion . . . Do you have a lil more of that tocktail?"

Simon figured that Mr. Thoat had already absorbed about four and a half ounces of vodka under the heading of the "couple of other things" in his concoction, and he did not want to overdo it.

"I've got something else, a Sanitade punch, to go with the salad," he said. "And I think we ought to be starting on it. I don't want to make you late."

Selina Thoat was bringing in the salad, and Simon went to the refrigerator for the punch. In this the motive power consisted of rum and gin, but in milder dilution with Sanitade and pineapple juice than the alcohol in the cocktail. Their necessary aroma was masked by liberal twists of orange peel, and the strength was carefully calculated to counteract the sobering effect of food and keep the consumer at the elevation he started at, without boosting him to a more dangerous altitude.

Mr. Thoat talked garrulously, often boastfully, and with many stumbles of enunciation which sometimes seemed to puzzle him, about his past achievements and future projects; Simon made the essential minimum of admiring and encouraging noises to keep him going; and Selina spent most of the time staring at the Saint with bewilderedly enlarged and rapturous eyes while she chewed her cud, which gave her a disconcerting resemblance to a lovesick cow. A preposterously long time seemed to crawl by before a clock struck two and Simon could initiate the adjournment.

"I'll do the dishes," volunteered Selina, "while you and Papa wash your hands."

Simon tidied the dining-living-room, thankful that there had been no smoking to add its problems of tell-tale ashes and odours, and joined Selina in the kitchen while Mr. Thoat was completing the euphemistic lavage. He was glad to see that she had cleaned up as meticulously as her upbringing would have predicted—he only wanted to be sure that an inoffensive earl would find no trace of vandalism, and might even staunchly deny that anyone could have used his flat in the way that Mr. Thoat might subsequently claim that it had been used.

Selina Thoat, however, was ruminating a different idea.

"If your servant has the day off," she said, "would you like me to come back and cook dinner for you?"

"You're very kind," said the Saint. "But I'm having dinner with a business associate, who's taking me to the airport."

"When you come back, then. Any Sunday when you're alone. Just call me."

"Thank you," said the Saint, and was able to sound more grateful because Mr. Thoat returned at that moment. "But now you really must be going."

He herded them to the door, picking up the deeds from the coffee-table on the way.

"You won't want to have this stuff bulging out of your pockets in the parade," he said. "Let me mail you your copy."

"You are mos' conshidrate, Mr. Tombs," Mr. Thoat said portentously. He amplified the thought, with an air of inspiration: "You have cast your bread upon the warrers. It will come back to you in good measure, preshed down an' run over."

He essayed a courtly bow, lurched a little, and proceeded down the stairs with extreme precision.

The deputation of Angels of Abstinence was already marshalled in military formation when Mr. Thoat and Selina located them in the irregular column of demonstrators which blocked half the old Carriage Road on the east of Park Lane. While they waited for the promenade to get under way, they were ringing the welkin with a song which Mr. Thoat himself had authored, to an accompaniment of drums, bazookas, and harmonicas played by the more talented members of the party:

> *"The little lambs so frisky,*
> *The birds who charm our ear,*
> *Have never tasted whisky,*
> *Or rum or gin or beer!"*

Emotionally stirred to the depths of his soul by the familiar melody and the uplifting words, Mr. Thoat was moved as he approached to adopt the role of conductor, waving his arms with an ecstatic exuberance that could only have been surpassed by Leonard Bernstein. The fact that this change of balance almost made him trip over his own feet he attributed to the unevenness of the ground.

"There he is," said Constable Yelland excitedly, standing in the fringe of the spectators in his best Sunday suit, beside an older man in somewhat plainer clothes on which the brand of Sir Robert Peel was nevertheless almost legible.

"Him?" said the Scotland Yard man, half incredulously. "I thought he was one of the top teetotallers."

Isaiah Thoat, suffused with a delirious sense of power

which he attributed to the encouraging smiles of his flock,
led them more vehemently into another stanza :

> *"Let's raise no girls and boys on*
> *Such filthy things to drink!*
> *Let's seize this cursèd poison*
> *And pour it down the sink!"*

"Boom-boom-boo-rah," added Mr. Thoat, stamping
his feet up and down in a martial manner; at which point
the Scotland Yard man tapped him on the shoulder and
presented himself with the time-honoured introduction.

"And I have a warrant for your arrest on a charge of
receiving stolen goods knowing the same to have been
stolen. It is my duty to warn you——"

"Ridiclush," said Mr. Thoat, leaning on him heavily.
"I'll report you to your shuprir offcer. Why, do you
know, I've jus' bin incrusted with a trush fund . . .
lemme tell you . . ."

Simon Templar had followed at a very discreet distance, merely to make sure that nothing remediable went
wrong with the situation on which he had toiled so honestly. But even at that range he was able to appreciate the
extra bulge of Selina Thoat's bovine eyes as she recognized Constable Yelland even in his horrible tailoring, and
flung her arms around his neck.

"My dream man," she moaned.

The standard-bearer of Scotland Yard was sniffing
Isaiah Thoat at almost equally close quarters, and his
verdict was fast and seasoned.

"He's reeking of it—rum, whisky, and I don't know
what else. She must be the same. Probably celebrating the
haul they made. We'd better take 'em both in. Blow your
whistle, stupid!"

THE UNCURED HAM

Once upon a time there was in Sweden a *Stallmästar*, a master of the royal stables, whose lodge and dependencies were situated at the edge of a wooded park and a pretty lake only two miles north of the centre of Stockholm. But even as far back as the middle of the seventeenth century such a choice location could not escape the covetous attention of more mercenary enterprise, and he was abruptly dispossessed in favour of an inn which, while still commemorating him sentimentally by calling itself *Stallmästaregården*, today features the hors d'oeuvre table instead of the horse trough.

Once upon a much later time there was a thief in the United States who would have preferred to be an actor—or, if he had been given his own version, an actor who was forced by lack of appreciation to become a thief. His name was Ernest Moldys, and it was the opinion of every producer for whom he had auditioned that he was a very bad actor indeed. It was, however, the consensus of many police departments that he was an excellent appraiser of jewels and a first-class burglar of houses, apartments, and hotel suites. These contradictory assessments had never convinced him, or discouraged him from declaiming long passages of Shakespeare whenever he could command an audience, which was usually in some tavern where he was buying drinks. Surmises were less unanimous as to whether he was obsessed with The Theatre for its own sake, or whether he was more lured by the putative fringe benefits of the profession—the international glamour queens whom he would professionally embrace and publicly escort, the swooning fans who would offer him their all for an autograph. He was certainly a dedicated dazzler of girls, the younger and more innocent the better; in fact, it was his too brilliant fascination, seduction, impregnation, and desertion of a teen-age beauty whom he found in a drama school which had achieved what a dozen detective bureaux had failed to do and put him to flight across the Atlantic to settle tentatively in Sweden, a country which will not extradite Americans on such locally incomprehensible complaints.

Once upon a yet more recent time, Simon Templar, who was known in many circles but fortunately for him not everywhere as "The Saint", chanced to be dining at an adjacent table at *Stallmästaregården* on the same night as Ernest Moldys had elected to take fodder at that hostelry.

"What I want," said Mr. Moldys aggressively, "is some of these 'crayfters'. "

He was then still in his mid-thirties, and handsome enough in the pseudo-rugged way that appeals to advertising photographers commissioned to prove that even hairy-chested tattooed he-men can enjoy after-shave lotions. In lieu of personality he affected an aggressive manner developed from watching certain old television films and designed to impress his masculinity upon his consorts of the moment, whom he carefully selected for their youthful impressionability, like the round-faced flaxen-haired girl who accompanied him that evening.

"I am sorry," said the head waiter, "but the *kräftor* season does not begin until tomorrow."

Kräftor is the fresh-water crayfish which looks exactly like a four-inch miniature northern lobster, and which is one of the most prized delicacies of Swedish gastronomy.

"I told you that when I told you about them, Ernest,"

said the girl, who looked as if she should have been doing her homework instead of going to dinner with such an obviously raffish date.

"I bet you can get them in America any time—if anyone wants 'em," said Mr. Moldys, implying that few people would condescend to do so.

"In Sweden the season is very short," said the head waiter apologetically. "It is only one month, beginning tomorrow, August the eighth."

"So what? So I made a mistake in the date. But that's only a few hours away. What's the difference? Don't tell me you haven't got a stock in the kitchen right now, ready for opening day. So let's have some."

"I am sorry, but the law is very strict. We cannot serve *kräftor* before tomorrow."

Mr. Moldys glowered.

"That's why you'll be goddam squareheads all your lives," he said loudly.

The head waiter bowed icily and moved away, but Mr. Moldys continued to hold forth for some time on the shortcoming of Europe in general, Scandinavia in particular, and the Swedish nation especially, in a voice that was pitched for the attention not only of his companion but of half the other customers in the room. It went to the limits of embarrassment before he consented to let her soothe him, and switched on again the flashing smile for which too many foolish virgins had forgiven his tasteless tantrums.

Although Mr. Moldys tirelessly dramatized himself to an extent which had caused his privileged associates to nickname him "The Ham", it was one of his failings that he could not confine himself to the act of charm, but firmly believed that the paperback private-eye performance was even more important.

Simon Templar would have been glad to forget the foregoing exhibition as quickly as possible; but a hardly overstretched arm of coincidence encircling a comparatively small capital had him installed at a veranda table at lunch the very next day at the Restaurant Riche, which is one of the impeccably best in Stockholm, when it again scooped in Ernest Moldys, who was now bedazzling another potential juvenile delinquent with the same enticing figure and coloration as his admirer of the night before, but a slightly different facial arrangement.

By this time Mr. Moldys had lost interest in *kräftor* and wanted *smörgåsbord*, which he was told the restaurant was not serving that day.

"Are you nuts?" demanded Mr. Moldys indignantly. "All Swedish restaurants have smorgasbord. They do in America, anyway."

"In Sweden there was always *smörgåsbord* in the old days," said another head waiter politely. "But it is not so fashionable here any more. However, you are lucky. Today is the first day of the crayfish."

"Oh, we must have those, Ernest," said the nymphet. "They are wonderful——"

"I don't want any. I heard all about them yesterday, when I couldn't get any. Now I don't care if I never have one. I want smorgasbord."

"How about some herring, sir? We have several kinds, the same as you would find in a *smörgåsbord*."

"I had herring yesterday. I can't eat it every day. For Chrissake, can't you ever get anything you want, when you want it, in this broken-down country? I know backstreet delicatessens in New York that'd make this joint look sick."

Mr. Moldys was talking in the same intentionally public-address voice which he had used the night before;

and as he glanced around to observe what attention he was getting, he caught Simon Templar's analytical eye on him, and was vain enough to honestly believe that he recruited himself an ally by turning on a brilliantly comradely smile.

"You know what I mean, don't you?" he said. "I can see you've been around. All this olde-worlde tradition and doing everything by the book—they're so far back, they don't even know they've been left behind! Don't you lose your mind sometimes?"

"Sometimes, I wonder why the natives don't lose theirs," said the Saint calmly. "Considering some of the things they have to put up with."

Ernest Moldys stared at him for several seconds with a strangely increasing uncertainty, and finally threw down his napkin with thinly disguised petulance.

"Let's get out of here, you beautiful Viking, and see if we can't get what we want somewheres else."

Simon saw the head waiter pick up the reservation slip that had been on their table, and beckoned him.

"What was that charming character's name?"

"A Mr. Moldys." The man showed him the paper. "You did not know him?"

"I wouldn't want to," said the Saint.

But this became untrue an instant after he said it; for the name, combined with something that had been vaguely familiar about the face, suddenly rang a bell in the complex circuits of Simon Templar's memory, which absorbed every item of criminal intelligence that touched it like a sponge, but had to be prodded in sometimes peculiar ways to squeeze the information back out again.

At this moment he recalled certain facts about Ernest Moldys which made him want very much to know more. There were, for instance, some details about the suicide of

that sixteen-year-old starlet in Hollywood on which his
recollection was hazy, to say nothing of the exact terms of
a reward which had once been offered by the victims of
one of Mr. Moldys's more remunerative depredations.

The Saint did not ordinarily feel that his mission re-
quired him to administer personal correctives to obnoxious
American tourists whose misbehaviour could supply gra-
tuitous ammunition to the ever-watchful snipers at the
free world, but this was a case where natural impulse and
lofty objective combined irresistibly with sound business
practice. Once upon an earlier time the consequent leg
work might have seemed discouragingly long-drawn and
complicated, but in the age of electronic communications
and jet aircraft it was almost no effort at all to a man who
could sleep at any hour and altitude in a reclining seat
like a child in a cradle. The Saint, who had nothing else
planned for the week-end, merely took an S.A.S. plane
over the North Pole from Copenhagen to Los Angeles and
returned by the same route, with his errands accomplished, in less time than it took Lindbergh to hobble from
New York to Paris.

Ernest Moldys had done very well out of the last exer-
cises of his vocation, but he also had very expensive tastes.
These, like his other fickle appetites, were only partly
genuine, another large part being dictated by his own
conception of the way a stage or movie star such as he
should have been would live. But the resulting pattern
had made alarmingly rapid inroads on the folios of American Express travellers' checks into which he had contrived
to convert most of his loot, and he only knew one trade
that was likely to replenish them.

Therefore he listened with guarded but lively interest
one evening when he was having a cocktail by himself in
the bar of the Grand Hotel, and a tall and vaguely pirati-

cal-looking individual whose features were recently familiar came in with an older man who wore his dark suit and bifocals with the unmistakable patina of a high-priced attorney, and after ordering a couple of Peter Dawsons on the rocks they continued what must have been a lengthily waged discussion.

"What burns me," said the Saint, "is that this harpy tells the court she needs all that alimony just to live on, in the style to which I've accustomed her. And she gets it. I have to pay her a company president's income just to feed and clothe her, supposedly. And the next thing I know, she's financing a season of Shakespeare. Well, if she can afford that, she obviously doesn't need all that money to live on, and we ought to be able to get it reduced."

"I know how you feel, Mr. Hurley," said the legal type. "But it's her income now, and she can do what she likes with it."

"If she wants to play at being a producer, she could cash in some of her jewels. Must be more than a quarter of a million dollars I spent on them—and of course she kept 'em all. There was ninety thousand just for a string of little rocks to hang where she should have a rope. Why doesn't she hock them for capital?"

"They were part of the divorce settlement, Mr. Hurley. There's no law that says she has to dig into her capital for anything she can pay for out of income."

"Does that include gigolos? This big nance that she's backing—with my money—nobody ever heard of him before. But she's going to make him a star. Even a California divorce-court judge couldn't be stupid enough not to see that she must have some other motive besides giving young genius a break."

"But you yourself called him a 'big nance'—and that's

pretty common gossip. You don't seriously think you could convince anyone that they were having an affair."

"Frankly, that part of it baffles me. Enid has always been queer for actors, but at least she only flipped for the virile kind. When the next one of those comes along, that queen is going to wonder what hit him."

"Perhaps you should look forward to that, Mr. Hurley. She might marry the next one, if he's virile enough."

"She'd never be stupid enough to do that unless he earned more than she's getting from me. Not that that'd stop her having her fun . . . It still gripes me. Enid Hurley, the great impresario, preparing to stand Copenhagen on its ear, dazzling 'em with my diamonds, taking over Kronborg Castle, yet, with my money!"

"Try not to think about it. Go down to Cannes and look at the bikinis."

"That's not what I interrupted your vacation for. I want you to try and *do* something."

"I've told you——"

"But she doesn't have a lawyer here, telling her. Go to Copenhagen and see her. Bluff her. Try to throw a scare into her. Tell her we're going to court to ask for a revision of the settlement. Tell her this proves she doesn't need so much alimony, which tell her the Court wouldn't give her for immoral purposes like subsidizing this swishy ham. Dress it up in all the phony legal gobbledygook, and if you do it well enough you might worry the hell out of her. Then offer to call it off if she'll agree to accept a nice fat cut."

"I don't think you've got a chance."

"Well, let *me* take that chance, will you? I can't let it go without trying. You might be able to convince her that she stands a good chance of ending up with nothing, if she fights it. She might even be tried for perjury or promoting vice or something. The arguments are your business. You'll be paid for it."

"It's not that I mind earning a fee, Mr. Hurley, but I can't conscientiously encourage you to spend your money with such a small prospect of getting anything in return."

"I'd rather do that than give it all to Enid without a struggle. And if you do swing it, you can bill me for a twenty-thousand-dollar bonus."

"Well," said the lawyer, glancing at his watch, "let's go to lunch and see if we can't improve our case just a little."

They paid their bill and departed, leaving Mr. Moldys with his ears still tingling, but not from the traditional eavesdropper's embarrassment. It was, rather, a warm glow of satisfaction that they had served him well, with a not inconsiderable assist from some possible guardian devil—a sensation that harmonized well with an equally symbolic itching of the fingers.

Mrs. Enid Hurley, a rich divorcée with jewels and a weakness for actors—it was a situation that might have been made for him. The only thought that failed to occur to him was that it had.

About all that was left for him to find out for himself was the name of the hotel where this pre-cooked goose was laying its golden eggs, and in a city as small as Copenhagen this would normally have taken no more than a few phone calls after his arrival. For him, the catastrophic obstacle was in the word "arrival". The cynical counsellor who had advised him to take a cure overseas had handed him, for a disproportionate fee, a list of countries warranted to be salubrious for his ailment; but Denmark was not one of them. And thus, after only a few minutes' contemplation of this windfall that had been so extravagantly dumped in his lap, he found himself glaring at it with the obsessive acerbity of a shark which has discovered a succulent skin-diver cavorting in its dining depths, only to learn from an unpredicted bump on the nose that this mouth-watering morsel is protected inside a plastic bubble installed by the anti-shark experts of some camera crew shooting scenes for another submarine superscoop.

What this trauma might have done to the psyche of Ernest Moldys (he had tried to crash the marquees with more euphonious and star-sounding appellations, but had lately settled on the theory of honest down-to-earthiness: if Ernest Borgnine could win Academy Awards and Ernest Hemingway could cop Pulitzer Prizes, who could make cracks about Ernest Moldys?) is an interesting speculation, but it was not put to the final test, for after three days and nights of agonized frustration his sufferings were ended by precisely the kind of miracle he had been reduced to dreaming about.

As he entered his hotel and headed for the desk to ask for his key that auspicious afternoon, a woman hurried in front of him with a preoccupied flash of apology and commanded the attention of the uniformed incumbent with the bulldozing confidence of five generations of spoiled American wives behind her.

"I'm Mrs. Hurley," she proclaimed, with the clarity of royalty announcing itself. "Have you got me a driver yet?"

"A driver, Mrs. Hurley?" The attendant looked blank. "What kind of driver did you want?"

"Do I have to go over all that again? I told you last night——"

"I was not on duty last night, madame."

"Well, whoever was here on the desk. I told him I needed someone to drive my car to Hälsingborg tomorrow, and he promised me he'd arrange it."

The attendant thumbed through a large ledger of

scrawled notes, and began a muttered consultation with an assistant; and the woman looked at Moldys again.

"I'm sorry—don't let me hold you up. This is obviously going to take time!"

He gave her the most dazzlingly good-natured smile that he could achieve with his heart in his mouth, without letting it fall out. He was so staggered by his good fortune that he almost lost all the *savoir-faire* on which he prided himself.

"Please—I'm not in any hurry."

"This is so aggravating. I thought I'd drive across from Hälsingborg and see some of the country, instead of flying, so yesterday I have to slip in the bathtub and fall down and crack my wrist." She raised a left hand which protruded from a small cast which had been hidden by the foulard sling in which she carried it. "Now I've got the problem of taking my car back. I suppose I *could* get along by myself somehow, but I might get into trouble, and it seems foolish to take a chance."

"I am sorry, madame," said the man behind the desk, "but I can find nothing about a driver. Perhaps when the night porter comes on duty——"

"But if I'm going to leave at all, I've got to leave first thing in the morning. If he hasn't done anything about it, somebody else had better get on the ball. Are you sure you looked under the right name? It's H—U—R—L—E—Y. Mrs. *Enid* Hurley."

"Yes, madame. But there is nothing here. Would you like me to try to find you a driver?"

At long last, Ernest Moldys regained full possession of his wits, and simultaneously of his voice. Although he was still finding it hard to believe that this was not all a wonderful dream, he knew exactly what had to be done and how to do it.

"Mrs. Hurley," he said, "if you won't think I'm being presumptuous, you have no problem. I'd be honoured if you'd let me drive you to wherever you were going."

"Oh, but I couldn't possibly take up your time !"

Thus, after a little perfunctory argument and an interval of a few hours, she was seated with him at a window table on the Strand Hotel's roof terrace, overlooking the lights of half the city, while they toasted each other in various experimental flavours of *brännvin* over the prawn pancakes and debated amiably on the merits of each. It was not even an ordeal for Mr. Moldys, for although she was considerably older than his usual choice, she was in such a superbly groomed and pampered state of preservation that she did not look a day older than himself. She had classic features and a *Vogue*-model figure, and her personality would have made the local chick whom he had sidetracked for the occasion look insipid beside her.

The only fault he had to find was that the diamonds he had heard so much about were not in evidence. As if sensing something critical in the way he had studied her evening finery, she fingered the costume necklace and bracelet set she was wearing, and said : "I'm afraid I'm not very dressy, for a place like this. But I only came for a couple of days, and since I was driving alone it didn't seem very smart to load all my baubles in the car, so I left them in the hotel safe in Copenhagen."

Moldys gallantly concealed his disappointment, although it seemed as if the luck which he thought had changed was turning dangerously coy again.

"A woman like you doesn't need jewels as much as they need her," he said, omitting to credit the writer from whom he had swiped the line.

Later in the meal, he learned for the first time that Hälsingborg, their destination on the west coast of Swed-

en, lay only two and a half miles across a narrow strait
from the similarly named Danish town of Helsingör,
which was practically a suburb of Copenhagen, a mere
thirty miles from the Danish capital.

"Both sides used to be fortified," explained Mrs. Hurley,
"and King Erik of Pomerania, who owned all the Scandi-
navian countries too, in those days, five or six hundred
years ago, charged a toll on all the ships going through the
Sound. It must have been quite a racket, because when
Frederik II got to be King of Denmark he rebuilt the fort
on his side into a fancy castle which he called Kronborg.
It was finished about 1585, only fifteen years before
Shakespeare wrote *Hamlet* and made it the scene of a
practically prehistoric legend. That's what they call poetic
licence, I guess."

"You sound as if you'd made a real study of it," he said
admiringly.

"Well, naturally I'm interested. You see, I'm putting on
a production of *Hamlet* there—of course, Helsingör is the
place that Shakespeare called 'Elsinore'."

"What a wonderful idea, to do *Hamlet* right in the very
place where it happened!"

"It probably never happened at all, and it certainly
couldn't have happened there, as I've told you. But even
the Danes have probably convinced themselves by now
that it did. It isn't a new idea to put on the play there—
people have been doing it since 1816. The challenge is to
do it better."

"You know, I'd never have taken you for a producer."

"Because I'm not chewing a cigar? But I'm as tough as
any of them, I hope."

"I refuse to believe it. At least, not like most of the ones
I came across."

"Don't tell me you're an actor!"

"I used to be, sort of." He was ad-libbing furiously now, not sure where he was going, but inspiredly sure that he was on the right track. "Nothing very important, you know. But some kind critics predicted a great future for me."

"What did you do?"

"I quit while I was ahead. I was on the verge of getting somewhere, when I inherited quite a bit of money, and the incentive to keep struggling was gone. But even now I can feel what it would mean to speak those lines in the place that Shakespeare himself was actually thinking of."

"Lots of 'em have done it—from Sir Laurence Olivier, way back in 1937 with Vivien Leigh, to Sir John Gielgud in '39, Sir Michael Redgrave in 1950, and Richard Burton in '54. He doesn't need to be knighted since they made him the King in *Camelot*. But I still see the part differently from any of them."

Mr. Moldys saluted her with another heartening measure of aromatic alcohol followed by the traditional beer chaser, and said:

"This above all: to thine own self be true,
And it must follow, as the night the day,
Thou canst not then be false to any man."

She looked at him with thoughtful interest.

"That was a nice reading," she said. "I've always thought Hamlet should be played something like *you* would naturally do it—as a real he-man trying to break out of a neurotic tradition, not a tormented introvert himself."

"Thus conscience does make cowards of us all," he said.
"And thus the native hue of resolution
Is sicklied o'er with the pale cast of thought."

"Exactly," she agreed. "Now, I've got a young actor

who's physically just the way I visualize a Hamlet type, but temperamentally I'm beginning to worry about him."

Moldys was astute enough not to crowd his luck any harder at that moment, and in any case he wanted time to decide what to drive for. But he was exultantly certain that he had made a tremendous impression, and it was unthinkable that such a sequence of breaks could fail to climax somehow in a perfect pay-off.

The Saint had a privileged insight into that psychology, having been the subject of it on several occasions himself.

Moldys played it with creditable restraint for the rest of the evening and through the following day's long drive, devoting as much time as possible to the rôle of intelligent listener, sympathetic but disinterested, agreeable but authoritative, which demanded a minimum of effort but gave him the maximum space in which to wait for the decisive opening.

But in spite of all that, when they sat at dinner again the following night on the terrace of the newly completed Kärnan Hotel on the sea front of Hälsingborg, he began to experience some of the classic emotions of the mythical giant Tantalus (of whom he personally had never heard) whose name is immortalized in the word "tantalize", whose doom it was to be parched by eternal thirst while chained beside a pool which always playfully receded a millimetre beyond the utmost reach of his tongue. He had even developed a confident belief that he was attractive to her on the most downright sexual plane, and that was an angle from which he knew unlimited approaches. But between consummation and salvation, between all his tactical advances and her jewels, still lay those two-and-a-half-miles of international water and the whimsies of international treaties. His lawyer, who was highly conscientious

within his limits, had been most insistent on those
technicalities.

Thus they looked at each other in a farewell atmosphere
across a table which commanded the narrow strait sepa-
rating them from the romantic turrets of Kronborg Castle,
which was accommodatingly floodlit, and sighed with
appropriate appreciation, and she could say : "I just hope
everything will work out all right. I'm taking on such a
big thing on my own. I mustn't even begin to doubt what
I'm doing."

Ernest Moldys took a big chance, from desperation, and
leaned forward to try another quote, in his best voice:

"Doubt thou the stars are fire,
Doubt that the sun doth move,
Doubt truth to be a liar,
    But never doubt I love——"

"You must believe in what you're doing, Mrs. Hurley,"
he covered himself hastily.

"Sometimes that isn't so easy." She continued to stare
at him with an air of discovery. "I talk very big and
independent, but it's a lonely business."

"I'll be waiting to read the notices, and I'm sure they'll
be great."

"Don't talk as if you'd be a million miles away. You've
got to come to the opening. In fact, since you've come this
far, why don't you come over with me and see what we're
doing?"

"I can't." He had to think of a reason quickly, and
perhaps automatically clutched at a recent memory for
inspiration. "My attorney is arriving from New York tomorrow to see me about some important business, and I
must be back in Stockholm to meet him."

She grimaced.

"Don't talk to me about lawyers—I left Copenhagen to

get away from one who was trying to blackmail me, in a strictly professional way. Packed an overnight bag and drove on to the ferry at Helsingör without telling anyone where I was going. I'm hoping by this time he'll've gotten tired of cooling his heels in my hotel waiting for me to come back."

Unlike Moldys, she did not have to improvise any of her explanations, for the creation of cover stories was one of the Saint's greatest specialities, and when he had polished one there was seldom a crevice in it for any question that had not been anticipated and prepared for.

He found her more attractive than ever that night, even if his primary impetus was provided by the magnetism of the diamonds which still reposed in a hotel safe a few infinite miles away, and his wooing might have become troublesome if she had not been able to plead that her cracked wrist was aching and throbbing in a way that would have completely inhibited her from responding with all the enthusiasm that such an occasion deserved. The Saint had not overlooked that hazard either.

The restless night that Moldys spent, however, was due to less romantic discouragement. In spite of all the auspices, the chariot of fortune seemed to have ended its delirious gallop in a morass of pure glue.

He was finishing a gloomy breakfast in the dining-room next morning when Enid Hurley came in, and even across the room her face told him that something new and dire had been added to the situation.

"You'll never guess," she said incontrovertibly, as she reached his table.

"What?"

"You remember that lawyer I mentioned last night? Well, he was hired by my ex-husband to pester me. So this morning I thought, before I actually went back, it might be smart to call my secretary in Copenhagen and find out if he was still hanging around. And you know what I find out?"

"No."

"He's gone, all right. But while I've been away, since he couldn't work on me, it seems he went to work on my actor, and got him so scared that he's quit and flown back to Hollywood. So here I am, scheduled for an opening in ten days, with no leading man."

"That's terrible," said Moldys uncertainly.

"It's worse than that! It's such a cheap victory for that bastard I was married to. He's made me look ridiculous in front of the whole world. And there's nothing I can do about it. You don't replace a sensational Hamlet over-night."

She stared at him as if she was going to burst into tears. But instead of saline solution, her eyes slowly filled with a strange inspirational light. Suddenly she pointed a finger like a sword.

"You," she breathed.

"What?" said Ernest Moldys, drawing a total blank in what should have been his climactic moment.

"You could play Hamlet," she said. "The way I visualized it. Better than that weak-kneed fop who walked out. You *must* do it, Ernest!"

Moldys moistened his lips and swallowed hard to hold down his bouncing aorta. He had a buzzing in his ears and a feeling of vertigo that made him hold on to the table to keep the room from spinning.

It is not for nothing that an over-enthusiastic actor is vulgarly referred to as a "ham". In the opinion of this etymologist, the term has neither anatomical nor dietetic connotations, but is simply an abbreviation of "Hamlet", the part which supposedly symbolizes the pinnacle of his-

trionic ambition. And if the perfect illustration of this
theory were called for, no better example could be cited
than Mr. Ernest Moldys.

And now it seemed as if the miracle in which he had
almost lost faith had at the last moment answered its last
mysterious cue and handed him the ultimate rôle on what
would have been conventionally called a silver platter by
anyone who was not more practically fascinated by its
incrustation of diamonds.

"You must do it," Enid Hurley was pleading. "For me.
You can start rehearsing tomorrow. You know the lines
already, I'm sure. You can phone your attorney in Stockholm, and tell him to fly over and meet you in Copenhagen instead. If it means any extra expense, I'll take care
of it. Between us, we'll show 'em. Please, Ernest, tell me
you will!"

With her impassioned eagerness and stark-naked need,
it was not hard for Mr. Moldys to forget that she was a
comparatively old bag. Perhaps, he reflected (if he was
capable just then of reflecting so coherently) he had too
long been squandering his talent for seduction. At any
rate, with everything else considered, the prospective
change of pace was in no way deterrent.

Rising at last to his moment of truth, he leaned forward
and covered her hand caressingly.

"Enid," he said, "for you, I'll do it. *'The play's the
thing——'*"

Simon Templar was unable this time to take the usual
bows for the script he had written, because he thought it
advisable to stay well out of sight until Ernest Moldys was
far off the ferry and irrevocably committed to Danish soil.

Moldys was allowed to drive a little way from the dock

before a uniformed guard stopped him and asked for his passport.

The guard handed the passport to a large dour individual in plain clothes who loomed up behind him.

At the same moment, a spectacled American-legal type whom Moldys abruptly recognized appeared on the other side of the car and opened the door. Before he had finished resolving the conclusion that this could only be the attorney of Mrs. Hurley's ex-husband who had not given up after all but had been lying in wait with some new scheme of harassment, Mrs. Hurley had slipped nimbly out of the adjoining seat and was hurrying away, with the supposed pestering lawyer making no attempt to detain or follow her.

The plain-clothes man put the passport in his pocket and said stiffly: "Mr. Moldys, I am of the Danish State Police. We have been asked by the American Government to hold you for extradition. You are under arrest."

The American lawyer leaned over to exhibit an identification card in a small plastic case. It bore his photograph and the insignia of the Department of Justice. He said: "I expect I'll be taking you back, Hambo."

Mr. Moldys was too devastated even to feel insulted. "Who set me up?" he croaked.

"I don't know what you're talking about," said the Federal agent virtuously.

Ernest Moldys would have been prematurely enlightened if he had witnessed the reunion of Mrs. Hurley with the piratical-looking man who had last been heard speaking of her so vindictively, around the corner of an adjacent building.

"You must have been magnificent," Simon Templar said, and hugged her. "At this point I've a good mind to bow out and let you collect all of the reward."

"I wouldn't want that," she said. "I only tried to lead up to everything exactly the way you coached me. I never thought I could do it. I told you I never did any professional acting myself. It was my daughter who had all the talent. I'm the one who'd be very happy to bow out now."

The Saint shook his head.

"I'm afraid that's impossible. You'll certainly have to testify on the charges involving her. And frankly, it should be worth something to see the Ham's performance when he finds out why he shouldn't have avoided meeting the parents of that girl in the drama school that he gave such a shoddy deal to. At the very least, he would have known your real name was different from the stage label she was using."

THE CONVENIENT MONSTER

"OF *courrse*," said Inspector Robert Mackenzie, of the Inverness-shire Constabulary, with a burr as broad as his boots seeming to add an extra *r* to the word, "I know ye're only in Scotland as an ordinary visitor, and no' expectin' to be mixed up in any criminal business."

"That's right," said the Saint cheerfully.

He was so used to this sort of thing that the monotony sometimes became irritating, but Inspector Mackenzie made the conventional gambit with such courteous geniality that it almost sounded like an official welcome. He was a large and homely man with large red hands and small twinkling grey eyes and sandy hair carefully plastered over the bare patch above his forehead, and so very obviously and traditionally a policeman that Simon Templar actually felt a kind of nostalgic affection for him. Short of a call from Chief Inspector Claud Eustace Teal in person, nothing could have brought back more sharply what the Saint often thought of as the good old days; and he took it as a compliment that even after so many years, and even as far away as Scotland itself, he was not lost to the telescopic eye of Scotland Yard.

"And I suppose," Mackenzie continued, "ye couldna even be bothered with a wee bit of a local mystery."

"What's your problem?" Simon asked. "Has somebody stolen the haggis you were fattening for the annual Police Banquet?"

The Inspector ignored this with the same stony dignity

with which he would have greeted the hoary question about what a Scotsman wore under his kilt.

"It might be involvin' the Loch Ness Monster," he said with the utmost gravity. "Nae doot ye've hairrd of that."

"All right," said the Saint good-humouredly. "I started this. I suppose I had it coming. But you're the first policeman who ever tried to pull my leg. Didn't they tell you that I'm the guy who's supposed to do the pulling?"

"I'm no' makin' a joke," Mackenzie persisted, aggrievedly, and the Saint stared at him.

It was in the spring of 1933 that a remarkable succession of sober and reputable witnesses began to testify that they had seen in Loch Ness a monstrous creature whose existence had been a legend of the region since ancient times, but which few persons in this century had claimed to have seen for themselves. The descriptions varied in detail, as human observations are prone to do, but they seemed generally to agree that the beast was roughly thirty feet long and could swim at about the same number of miles per hour; it was a dark grey in colour, with a small horse-like head on a long tapering neck, which it turned from side to side with the quick movements of an alert hen. There were divergencies as to whether it had one or more humps in its back, and whether it churned the water with flippers or a powerful tail; but all agreed that it could not be classified with anything known to modern natural history.

The reports culminated in December with a photograph showing a strange reptilian shape thrashing in the water, taken by a senior employee of the British Aluminium Company, which has a plant near by. A number of experts certified the negative to be unretouched and unfaked, and the headline writers took it from there.

Within a fortnight, a London newspaper had a correspondent on the scene with a highly publicized big-game authority in tow; some footprints were found and casts made of them—which before the New Year was three days old had been pronounced by the chief zoologists of the British Museum to have all been made by the right hind foot of a hippopotamus, and a stuffed hippopotamus at that. In the nation wide guffaw which followed the exposure of this hoax, the whole matter exploded into a theme for cartoonists and comedians, and that aura of hilarious incredulity still coloured the Saint's vague recollections of the subject.

It took a little while for him to convince himself that the Inspector's straight face was not part of an elaborate exercise in Highland humour.

"What has the Monster done that's illegal?" Simon inquired at length, with a gravity to match Mackenzie's own.

"A few weeks ago, it's thocht to ha' eaten a sheep. And last night it may ha' killed a dog."

"Where was this?"

"The sheep belonged to Fergus Clanraith, who has a farm by the loch beyond Foyers, and the dog belongs to his neighbours, a couple named Bastion from doon in England who settled here last summer. 'Tis only aboot twenty miles away, if ye could spairr the time to run doon the road with me."

The Saint sighed. In certain interludes, he thought that everything had already happened to him that could befall a man with his exceptional gift for stumbling into fantastic situations and being offered bizarre assignments, but apparently there was always some still more preposterous imbroglio waiting to entangle him.

"Okay," he said resignedly. "I've been slugged with practically every other improbability you could raise an eyebrow at, so why should I draw the line at dog-slaying monsters. Lay on, Macduff."

"The name is Mackenzie," said the Inspector seriously.

Simon paid his hotel bill and took his own car, for he had been intending to continue his pleasantly aimless wandering that day anyhow, and it would not make much difference to him where he stopped along the way. He followed Mackenzie's somewhat venerable chariot out of Inverness on the road that takes the east bank of the Ness River, and in a few minutes the slaty grimness of the town had been gratefully forgotten in the green and gold loveliness of the countryside.

The road ran at a fairly straight tangent to the curves of the river and the Caledonian Canal, giving only infrequent glimpses of the seven locks built to lift shipping to the level of the lake, until at Dores he had his first view of Loch Ness at its full breadth.

The Great Glen of Scotland transects the country diagonally from northeast to southwest, as if a giant had tried to break off the upper end of the land between the deep natural notches formed by Loch Linnhe and the Beauly Firth. On the map which Simon had seen, the chain of lochs stretched in an almost crow-flight line that had made him look twice to be sure that there was not in fact a clear channel across from the Eastern to the Western Sea. Loch Ness itself, a tremendous trough twenty-four miles long but only averaging about a mile in width, suggested nothing more than an enlargement of the Canal system which gave access to it at both ends. But not many vessels seemed to avail themselves of the passage, for there was no boat in sight on the lake that afternoon. With the water as calm as a mill-pond and the fields and trees rising from its shores to a blue sky dappled with soft woolly clouds, it was as pretty as a picture postcard and utterly unconvincing to think of as a place which might be haunted by some outlandish horror from the mists of antiquity.

For a drive of twenty minutes, at the sedate pace set by Mackenzie, the highway paralleled the edge of the loch a little way up its steep stony banks. The opposite shore widened slightly into the tranquil beauty of Urquhart Bay with its ancient castle standing out grey and stately on the far point, and then returned to the original almost uniform breadth. Then, within fortunately brief sight of the unpicturesque aluminium works, it bore away to the south through the small stark village of Foyers and went winding up the glen of one of the tumbling streams that feed the lake.

Several minutes further on, Mackenzie turned off into a narrow side road that twisted around and over a hill and swung down again, until suddenly the loch was spread out squarely before them once more and the lane curled past the first of two houses that could be seen standing solitarily apart from each other but each within a bowshot of the loch. Both of them stood out with equal harshness against the gentle curves and colours of the landscape with the same dark graceless austerity as the last village or the last town or any other buildings Simon had seen in Scotland, a country whose unbounded natural beauty seemed to have inspired no corresponding artistry in its architects, but rather to have goaded them into competition to offset it with the most contrasting ugliness into which bricks and stone and tile could be assembled. This was a paradox to which he had failed to fit a plausible theory for so long that he had finally given up trying.

Beside the first house, a man in a stained shirt and corduroy trousers tucked into muddy canvas leggings was digging in a vegetable garden. He looked up as Mackenzie brought his rattletrap to a stop, and walked slowly over to the hedge. He was short but powerfully built, and his hair flamed like a stormy sunset.

Mackenzie climbed out and beckoned to the Saint. As Simon reached them, the red-haired man was saying: "Aye, I've been over and seen what's left o' the dog. It's more than they found of my sheep, I can tell ye."

"But could it ha' been the same thing that did it?" asked the Inspector.

"That's no' for me to say, Mackenzie. I'm no' a detective. But remember, it wasna me who said the Monster took my sheep. It was the Bastions who thocht o' that, it might be to head me off from askin' if *they* hadn't been the last to see it—pairhaps on their own Sunday dinner table. There's nae such trick I wouldna put beyond the Sassenach."

Mackenzie introduced them: "This is Mr. Clanraith, whom I was tellin' ye aboot. Fergus, I'd like ye to meet Mr. Templar, who may be helpin' me to investigate these goings-on."

Clanraith gave Simon a muscular and horny grip across the untrimmed hedge, appraising him shrewdly from under shaggy ginger brows.

"Ye dinna look like a policeman, Mr. Templar."

"I try not to," said the Saint expressionlessly. "Did you mean by what you were just saying that you don't believe in the Monster at all?"

"I didna say that."

"Then apart from anything else, you think there might actually be such a thing."

"There might."

"Living where you do, I should think you'd have as good a chance as anyone of seeing it yourself—if it does exist."

The farmer peered at Simon suspiciously.

"Wad ye be a reporrter, Mr. Templar, pairhaps?"

"No, I'm not," Simon assured him; but the other remained obdurately wary.

"When a man tells o' seein' monsters, his best friends are apt to wonder if he may ha 'taken a wee drop too much. If I had seen anything, ever, I wadna be talkin' aboot it to every stranger, to be made a laughin'-stock of."

"But ye'll admit," Mackenzie put in, "it's no' exactly norrmal for a dog to be chewed up an' killed the way this one was."

"I wull say this," Clanraith conceded guardedly. "It's strange that nobody hairrd the dog bark, or e'en whimper."

Through the Saint's mind flickered an eerie vision of something amorphous and loathsome oozing soundlessly out of night-blackened water, flowing with obscene stealth towards a hound that slept unwarned by any of its senses.

"Do you mean it mightn't've had a chance to let out even a yip?"

"I'm no' sayin'," Clanraith maintained cautiously. "But it was a guid watchdog, if naught else."

A girl had stepped out of the house and come closer while they talked. She had Fergus Clanraith's fiery hair and greenish eyes, but her skin was pink and white where his was weather-beaten and her lips were full where his were tight. She was half a head taller than he, and her figure was slim where it should be.

Now she said : "That's right. He even barked whenever he heard me coming, although he saw me every day."

Her voice was low and well modulated, with only an attractive trace of her father's accent.

"Then if it was a pairrson wha killed him, Annie, 'twad only mean it was a body he was still more used to."

"But you can't really believe that any human being

would do a thing like that to a dog that knew them—least of all to their own dog!"

"That's the trouble wi' lettin' a lass be brocht up an' schooled on the wrong side o' the Tweed," Clanraith said darkly. "She forgets what the English ha' done to honest Scotsmen no' so lang syne."

The girl's eyes had kept returning to the Saint with candid interest, and it was to him that she explained, smiling: "Father still wishes he could fight for Bonnie Prince Charlie. He's glad to let me do part-time secretarial work for Mr. Bastion because I can live at home and keep house as well, but he still feels I'm guilty of fraternizing with the Enemy."

"We'd best be gettin' on and talk to them ourselves," Mackenzie said. "And then we'll see if Mr. Templar has any more questions to ask."

There was something in Annie Clanraith's glance which seemed to say that she hoped that he would, and the Saint was inclined to be of the same sentiment. He had certainly not expected to find anyone so decorative in the cast of characters, and he began to feel a tentative quickening of optimism about this interruption in his travels. He could see her in his rear-view mirror, still standing by the hedge and following him with her gaze after her father had turned back to his digging.

About three hundred yards and a few bends farther on, Mackenzie veered between a pair of stone gateposts and chugged to a standstill on the circular driveway in front of the second house. Simon stopped behind him and then strolled after him to the front door, which was opened almost at once by a tall thin man in a pullover and baggy grey flannel slacks.

"Good afternoon, sir," said the detective courteously.

"I'm Inspector Mackenzie from Inverness. Are ye Mr. Bastion?"

"Yes."

Bastion had a bony face with a long aquiline nose, lank black hair flecked with grey, and a broad toothbrush moustache that gave him an indeterminately military appearance. His black eyes flickered to the Saint inquiringly.

"This is Mr. Templar, who may be assistin' me," Mackenzie said. "The constable who was here this morning told me all aboot what ye showed him, on the telephone, but could we hae a wee look for ourselves?"

"Oh, yes, certainly. Will you come this way?"

The way was around the house, across an uninspired formal garden at the back which looked overdue for the attention of a gardener, and through a small orchard beyond which a stretch of rough grass sloped quickly down to the water. As the meadow fell away, a pebbly beach came into view, and Simon saw that this was one of the rare breaches in the steep average angle of the loch's sides. On either side of the little beach the ground swelled up again to form a shallow bowl that gave an easy natural access to the lake. The path that they traced led to a short rustic pier with a shabby skiff tied to it, and on the ground to one side of the pier was something covered with potato sacking.

"I haven't touched anything, as the constable asked me," Bastion said. "Except to cover him up."

He bent down and carefully lifted off the burlap.

They looked down in silence at what was uncovered.

"The puir beastie," Mackenzie said at last.

It had been a large dog of confused parentage in which the Alsatian may have predominated. What had happened to it was no nicer to look at than it is to catalogue. Its head and hind quarters were partly mashed to a red pulp; and plainly traceable across its chest was a row of slot-like gashes, each about an inch long and close together, from which blood had run and clotted in the short fur. Mackenzie squatted and stretched the skin with gentle fingers to see the slits more clearly. The Saint also felt the chest: it had an unnatural contour where the line of punctures crossed it, and his probing touch found only sponginess where there should have been a hard cage of ribs.

His eyes met Mackenzie's across the pitifully mangled form.

"That would be quite a row of teeth," he remarked.

"Aye," said the Inspector grimly. "But what lives here that has a mouth like that?"

They straightened up and surveyed the immediate surroundings. The ground here, only a stride or two from the beach, which in turn was less than a yard wide, was so moist that it was soggy, and pockets of muddy liquid stood in the deeper indentations with which it was plentifully rumpled. The carpet of coarse grass made individual impressions difficult to identify, but three or four shoe-heel prints could be positively distinguished.

"I'm afraid I made a lot of those tracks," Bastion said. "I know you're not supposed to go near anything, but all I could think of at the time was seeing if he was still alive and if I could do anything for him. The constable tramped around a bit too, when he was here." He pointed past the body. "But neither of us had anything to do with those marks there."

Close to the beach was a place where the turf looked as if it had been raked by something with three gigantic claws. One talon had caught in the roots of a tuft of grass and torn it up bodily: the clump lay on the pebbles at the water's edge. Aside from that, the claws had left three parallel grooves, about four inches apart and each about half an inch wide. They dug into the ground at their upper ends to a depth of more than two inches, and dragged back towards the lake for a length of about ten inches as they tapered up.

Simon and Mackenzie stood on the pebbles to study the marks, Simon spanning them experimentally with his fingers while the detective took more exact measurements with a tape and entered them in his notebook.

"Anything wi' a foot big enough to carry claws like that," Mackenzie said, "I'd no' wish to ha' comin' after me."

"Well, they call it a Monster, don't they?" said the Saint dryly. "It wouldn't impress anyone if it made tracks like a mouse."

Mackenzie unbent his knees stiffly, shooting the Saint a distrustful glance, and turned to Bastion.

"When did ye find all this, sir?" he asked.

"I suppose it was about six o'clock," Bastion said. "I woke up before dawn and couldn't get to sleep again, so I decided to try a little early fishing. I got up as soon as it was light——"

"Ye didna hear any noise before that?"

"No."

"It couldna ha' been the dog barkin' that woke ye?"

"Not that I'm aware of. And my wife is a very light sleeper, and she didn't hear anything. But I was rather surprised when I didn't see the dog outside. He doesn't sleep in the house, but he's always waiting on the doorstep in the morning. However, I came on down here—and that's how I found him."

"And you didn't see anything else?" Simon asked. "In the lake, I mean."

"No. I didn't see the Monster. And when I looked for

it, there wasn't a ripple on the water. Of course, the dog may have been killed some time before, though his body was still warm."

"Mr. Bastion," Mackenzie said, "do *ye* believe it was the Monster that killed him?"

Bastion looked at him and at the Saint.

"I'm not a superstitious man," he replied. "But if it wasn't a monster of some kind, what else could it have been?"

The Inspector closed his notebook with a snap that seemed to be echoed by his clamping lips. It was evident that he felt that the situation was wandering far outside his professional province. He scowled at the Saint as though he expected Simon to do something about it.

"It might be interesting," Simon said thoughtfully, "if we got a vet to do a post-mortem."

"What for?" Bastion demanded brusquely.

"Let's face it," said the Saint. "Those claw marks *could* be fakes. And the dog *could* have been mashed up with some sort of club—even a club with spikes set in it to leave wounds that'd look as if they were made by teeth. But by all accounts, no one could have got near enough to the dog to do that without him barking. *Unless the dog was doped first.* So before we go overboard on this Monster theory, I'd like to rule everything else out. An autopsy would do that."

Bastion rubbed his scrubby moustache.

"I see your point. Yes, that might be a good idea."

He helped them to shift the dog on to the sack which had previously covered it, and Simon and Mackenzie carried it between them back to the driveway and laid it in the boot of the detective's car.

"D'ye think we could ha' a wurrd wi' Mrs. Bastion,

sir?" Mackenzie asked, wiping his hands on a clean rag
and passing it to the Saint.

"I suppose so," Bastion assented dubiously. "Although
she's pretty upset about this, as you can imagine. It was
really her dog more than mine. But come in, and I'll see
if she'll talk to you for a minute."

But Mrs. Bastion herself settled that by meeting them
in the hall, and she made it obvious that she had been
watching them from a window.

"What are they doing with Golly, Noel?" she greeted
her husband wildly. "Why are they taking him away?"

"They want to have him examined by a doctor, dear."

Bastion went on to explain why, until she interrupted
him again:

"Then don't let them bring him back. It's bad enough
to have seen him the way he is, without having to look at
him dissected." She turned to Simon and Mackenzie.
"You must understand how I feel. Golly was like a son to
me. His name was really Goliath—I called him that because he was so big and fierce, but actually he was a
pushover when you got on the right side of him."

Words came from her in a driving torrent that suggested
the corollary of a power-house. She was a big-boned
strong-featured woman who made no attempt to minimize
any of her probable forty-five years. Her blonde hair was
unwaved and pulled back into a tight bun, and her blue
eyes were set in a nest of wrinkles that would have been
called characterful on an outdoor man. Her lipstick, which
needed renewing, had a slapdash air of being her one
impatient concession to feminine artifice. But Bastion put
a soothing arm around her as solicitously as if she had
been a dimpled bride.

"I'm sure these officers will have him buried for us,

Eleanor," he said. "But while they're here I think they wanted to ask you something."

"Only to confairrm what Mr. Bastion told us, ma'm," said Mackenzie. "That ye didna hear any disturrbance last night."

"Absolutely not. And if Golly had made a sound, I should have heard him. I always do. Why are you trying so hard to get around the facts? It's as plain as a pikestaff that the Monster did it."

"Some monsters have two legs," Simon remarked.

"And I suppose you're taught not to believe in any other kind. Even with the evidence under your very eyes."

"I mind a time when some other footprints were found, ma'm," Mackenzie put in deferentially, "which turned oot to be a fraud."

"I know exactly what you're referring to. And that stupid hoax made a lot of idiots disbelieve the authentic photograph which was taken just before it, and refuse to accept an even better picture that was taken by a thoroughly reputable London surgeon about four months later. I know what I'm talking about. I've studied the subject. As a matter of fact, the reason we took this house was mainly because I'm hoping to discover the Monster."

Two pairs of eyebrows shot up and lowered almost in unison, but it was the Saint who spoke for Mackenzie as well as himself.

"How would you do that, Mrs. Bastion?" he inquired with some circumspection. "If the Monster has been well known around here for a few centuries, at least to everyone who believes in him——"

"It still hasn't been scientifically and officially established. I'd like to have the credit for doing that, beyond any shadow of doubt, and having it named *monstrum eleanoris*."

"Probably you gentlemen don't know it," Bastion elucidated, with a kind of quaintly protective pride, "but Mrs. Bastion is a rather distinguished naturalist. She's hunted every kind of big game there is, and even holds a couple of world's records."

"But I never had a trophy as important as this would be," his better half looked over again. "I expect you think I'm a little cracked—that there couldn't really be any animal of any size in the world that hasn't been discovered by this time. Tell them the facts of life, Noel."

Bastion cleared his throat like a schoolboy preparing to recite, and said with much the same awkward air: "The gorilla was only discovered in 1847, the giant panda in 1869, and the okapi wasn't discovered till 1901. Of course explorers brought back rumours of them, but people thought they were just native fairytales. And you yourselves probably remember reading about the first coelacanth being caught. That was only in 1938."

"So why shouldn't there still be something else left that I could be the first to prove?" Eleanor Bastion concluded for him. "The obvious thing to go after, I suppose, was the Abominable Snowman; but Mr. Bastion can't stand high altitudes. So I'm making do with the Loch Ness Monster."

Inspector Mackenzie, who had for some time been looking progressively more confused and impatient in spite of his politely valiant efforts to conceal the fact, finally managed to interrupt the antiphonal barrage of what he could only be expected to regard as delirious irrelevancies.

"All that I'm consairrned wi', ma'm," he said heavily, "is tryin' to detairrmine whether there's a human felon to be apprehended. If it should turrn oot to be a monster, as ye're thinkin', it wadna be in my jurisdeection. However, in that case, pairhaps Mr. Templar, who is no' a police officer, could be o' more help to ye."

"Templar," Bastion repeated slowly. "I feel as if I ought to recognize that name, now, but I was rather preoccupied with something else when I first heard it."

"Do you have a halo on you somewhere?" quizzed Mrs. Bastion, the huntress, in a tone which somehow suggested the aiming of a gun.

"Sometimes."

"Well, by Jove!" Bastion said. "I should've guessed it, of course, if I'd been thinking about it. You didn't sound like a policeman."

Mackenzie winced faintly, but both the Bastions were too openly absorbed in re-appraising the Saint to notice it.

Simon Templar should have been hardened to that kind of scrutiny, but as the years went on it was beginning to cause him a mixture of embarrassment and petty irritation. He wished that new acquaintances could dispense with the reactions and stay with their original problems.

He said, rather roughly: "It's just my bad luck that Mackenzie caught me as I was leaving Inverness. I was on my way to Loch Lomond, like any innocent tourist, to find out how bonnie the banks actually are. He talked me into taking the low road instead of the high road, and stopping here to stick my nose into your problem."

"But that's perfectly wonderful!" Mrs. Bastion announced like a bugle. "Noel, ask him to stay the night. I mean, for the week-end. Or for the rest of the week, if he can spare the time."

"Why-er-yes," Bastion concurred obediently. "Yes, of course. We'd be delighted. The Saint ought to have some good ideas about catching a monster."

Simon regarded him coolly, aware of the invisible glow of slightly malicious expectation emanating from Mackenzie, and made a reckless instant decision.

"Thank you," he said. "I'd love it. I'll bring in my things, and Mac can be on his way."

He sauntered out without further palaver, happily conscious that only Mrs. Bastion had not been moderately rocked by his casual acceptance.

They all ask for it, he thought. Cops and civilians alike, as soon as they hear the name. Well, let's oblige them. And see how they like whatever comes of it.

Mackenzie followed him outside, with a certain ponderous dubiety which indicated that some of the joke had already evaporated.

"Ye'll ha' no authorrity in this, ye underrstand," he emphasized, "except the rights o' any private investigator —which are no' the same in Scotland as in America, to judge by some o' the books I've read."

"I shall try very hard not to gang agley," Simon assured him. "Just phone me the result of the PM as soon as you possibly can. And while you're waiting for it, you might look up the law about shooting monsters. See if one has to take out a special licence, or anything like that."

He watched the detective drive away, and went back in with his suitcase. He felt better already, with no official eyes and ears absorbing his most trivial responses. And it would be highly misleading to say that he found the bare facts of the case, as they had been presented to him, utterly banal and boring.

Noel Bastion showed him to a small but comfortable room upstairs, with a window that faced towards the home of Fergus Clanraith but which also afforded a side-long glimpse of the loch. Mrs. Bastion was already busy there, making up the bed.

"You can't get any servants in a place like this," she explained. "I'm lucky to have a woman who bicycles up from Fort Augustus once a week to do the heavy cleaning.

They all want to stay in the towns where they can have what they think of as a bit of life."

Simon looked at Bastion innocuously and remarked:

"You're lucky to find a secretary right on the spot like the one I met up the road."

"Oh, you mean Annie Clanraith." Bastion scrubbed a knuckle on his upper lip. "Yes. She was working in Liverpool, but she came home at Christmas to spend the holidays with her father. I had to get some typing done in a hurry, and she helped me out. It was Clanraith who talked her into staying. I couldn't pay her as much as she'd been earning in Liverpool, but he pointed out that she'd end up with just as much in her pocket if she didn't have to pay for board and lodging, which he'd give her if she kept house. He's a widower, so it's not a bad deal for him."

"Noel's a writer," Mrs. Bastion said. "His big book isn't finished yet, but he works on it all the time."

"It's a life of Wellington," said the writer. "It's never been done, as I think it should be, by a professional soldier."

"Mackenzie didn't tell me anything about your background," said the Saint. "What should he have called you —Colonel?"

"Only Major. But that was in the Regular Army."

Simon did not miss the faintly defensive tone of the addendum. But the silent calculation he made was that the pension of a retired British Army major, unless augmented by some more commercial form of authorship than an unfinished biography of distinctly limited appeal, would not finance enough big-game safaris to earn an ambitious huntress a great reputation.

"There," said Mrs. Bastion finally. "Now if you'd like to settle in and make yourself at home, I'll have some tea ready in five minutes."

The Saint had embarked on his Scottish trip with an open mind and an attitude of benevolent optimism, but if anyone had prophesied that it would lead to him sipping tea in the drawing-room of two practically total strangers, with his valise unpacked in their guest bedroom, and solemnly chatting about a monster as if it were as real as a monkey, he would probably have been mildy derisive. His hostess, however, was obsessed with the topic.

"Listen to this," she said, fetching a well-worn volume from a bookcase. "It's a quotation from the biography of St Columba, written about the middle of the seventh century. It tells about his visit to Inverness some hundred years before, and it says *he was obliged to cross the water of Nesa; and when he had come to the bank he sees some of the inhabitants bringing an unfortunate fellow whom, as those who were bringing him related, a little while before some aquatic monster seized and savagely bit while he was swimming . . . . The blessed man orders one of his companions to swim out and bring him from over the water a coble. . . . Lugne Mocumin without delay takes off his clothes except his tunic and casts himself into the water. But the monster comes up and moves towards the man as he swam. . . . The blessed man, seeing it, commanded the ferocious monster saying 'Go thou no further nor touch the man; go back at once'. Then on hearing this word of the Saint the monster was terrified and fled away again more quickly than if it had been dragged off by ropes.*"

"I must try to remember that formula," Simon murmured, "and hope the monster can't tell one Saint from another."

" 'Monster' is really a rather stupid name for it," Mrs. Bastion said. "It encourages people to be illogical about it. Actually, in the old days the local people called it *an*

Niseag, which is simply the name 'Ness' in Gaelic with a feminine diminutive ending. You could literally translate it as 'Nessie'."

"That does sound a lot cuter," Simon agreed. "If you forget how it plays with dogs."

Eleanor Bastion's weathered face went pale, but the muscles under the skin did not flinch.

"I haven't forgotten Golly. But I was trying to keep my mind off him."

"Assuming this beastie does exist," said the Saint, "how did it get here?"

"Why did it have to 'get' here at all? I find it easier to believe that it always *was* here. The loch is 750 feet deep, which is twice the mean depth of the North Sea. *An Niseag* is a creature that obviously prefers the depths and only comes to the surface occasionally. I think its original home was always at the bottom of the loch, and it was trapped there when some prehistoric geological upheaval cut off the loch from the sea."

"And it's lived there ever since—for how many million years?"

"Not the original ones—I suppose we must assume at least a couple. But their descendants. Like many primitive creatures, it probably lives to a tremendous age."

"What do you think it is?"

"Most likely something of the plesiosaurus family. The descriptions sound more like that than anything—large body, long neck, paddle-like legs. Some people claim to have seen stumpy projections on its head, rather like the horns of a snail, which aren't part of the usual reconstruction of a plesiosaurus. But after all, we've never seen much of a plesiosaurus except its skeleton. You wouldn't know exactly what a snail looked like if you'd only seen its shell."

"But if Nessie has been here all this time, why wasn't she reported much longer ago?"

"She was. You heard that story about St Columba. And if you think only modern observations are worth paying attention to, several reliable sightings were recorded from 1871 onwards."

"But there was no motor road along the loch until 1933," Bastion managed to contribute at last, "and a trip like you made today would have been quite an expedition. So there weren't many witnesses about until fairly recently, of the type that scientists would take seriously."

Simon lighted a cigarette. The picture was clear enough. Like the flying saucers, it depended on what you wanted to believe—and whom.

Except that here there was not only fantasy to be thought of. There could be felony.

"What would you have to do to make it an official discovery?"

"We have movie and still cameras with the most powerful telephoto lenses you can buy," said the woman. "I spend eight hours a day simply watching the lake, just like anyone might put in at a regular job, but I vary the times of day systematically. Noel sometimes puts in a few hours as well. We have a view for several miles in both directions, and by the law of averages *an Niseag* must come up eventually in the area we're covering. Whenever that happens, our lenses will get close-up pictures that'll show every detail beyond any possibility of argument. It's simply a matter of patience, and when I came here I made up my mind that I'd spend ten years on it if necessary."

"And now," said the Saint, "I guess you're more convinced than ever that you're on the right track and the scent is hot."

Mrs. Bastion looked him in the eyes with terrifying equanimity.

"Now," she said, "I'm going to watch with a Weatherby Magnum as well as the cameras. *An Niseag* can't be much bigger than an elephant, and it isn't any more bullet-proof. I used to think it'd be a crime to kill the last survivor of a species, but since I saw what it did to poor Golly I'd like to have it as a trophy as well as a picture."

There was much more of this conversation, but nothing that would not seem repetitious in verbatim quotation. Mrs. Bastion had accumulated numerous other books on the subject, from any of which she was prepared to read excerpts in support of her convictions.

It was hardly 8:30, however, after a supper of cold meat and salad, when she announced that she was going to bed.

"I want to get up at two o'clock and be out at the loch well before daylight—the same time when that thing must have been there this morning."

"Okay," said the Saint. "Knock on my door, and I'll go with you."

He remained to accept a nightcap of Peter Dawson, which seemed to taste especially rich and smooth in the land where they made it. Probably this was his imagination, but it gave him a pleasant feeling of drinking the wine of the country on its own home ground.

"If you're going to be kind enough to look after her, I may sleep a bit later," Bastion said. "I must get some work done on my book tonight, while there's a little peace and quiet. Not that Eleanor can't take care of herself better than most women, but I wouldn't like her being out there alone after what's happened."

"You're thoroughly sold on this monster yourself, are you?"

The other stared into his glass.

"It's the sort of thing that all my instincts and experience would take with a grain of salt. But you've seen for yourself that it isn't easy to argue with Eleanor. And I must admit that she makes a terrific case for it. But until this morning I was keeping an open mind."

"And now it isn't so open?"

"Quite frankly, I'm pretty shaken. I feel it's got to be settled now, one way or the other. Perhaps you'll have some luck tomorrow."

It did in fact turn out to be a vigil that gave Simon goose-pimples, but they were caused almost entirely by the pre-dawn chill of the air. Daylight came slowly, through a grey and leaky-looking overcast. The lake remained unruffled, guarding its secrets under a pale pearly glaze.

"I wonder what we did wrong," Mrs. Bastion said at last, when the daylight was as broad as the clouds evidently intended to let it become. "The thing should have come back to where it made its last kill. Perhaps if we hadn't been so sentimental we should have left Golly right where he was and built a *machan* over him where we could have stood watch in turns."

Simon was not so disappointed. Indeed, if a monster had actually appeared almost on schedule under their expectant eyes, he would have been inclined to sense the hand of a Hollywood B-picture producer rather than the finger of Fate.

"As you said yesterday, it's a matter of patience," he observed philosophically. "But the odds are that the rest of your eight hours, now, will be just routine. So if you're not nervous I'll ramble around a while."

His rambling had brought him no nearer to the house than the orchard when the sight of a coppery-rosy head on top of a shapely free-swinging figure made his pulse fluctuate enjoyably with a reminder of the remotely possible promise of romantic compensation that had started to warm his interest the day before.

Annie Clanraith's smile was so eager and happy to see him that he might have been an old and close friend who had been away for a long time.

"Inspector Mackenzie told my father he'd left you here when he drove away. I'm so glad you stayed!"

"I'm glad you're glad," said the Saint, and against her ingenuous sincerity it was impossible to make the reply sound even vestigially sceptical. "But what made it so important?"

"Just having someone new and alive to talk to. You haven't stayed long enough to find out how bored you can be here."

"But you've got a job that must be a little more attractive than going back to an office in Liverpool."

"Oh, it's not bad. And it helps to make Father comfortable. And it's nice to live in such beautiful scenery, I expect you'll say. But I read books and I look at the TV, and I can't stop having my silly dreams."

"A gal like you," he said teasingly, "should have her hands full, fighting off other dreamers."

"All I get my hands full of is pages and pages of military strategy, about a man who only managed to beat Napoleon. But at least Napoleon had Josephine. The only thing Wellington gave his name to was an old boot."

Simon clucked sympathetically.

"He may have had moments with his boots off, you know. Or has your father taught you to believe nothing good of anyone who was ever born south of the Tweed?"

"You must have thought it was terrible, the way he

talked about Mr. Bastion. And he's so nice, isn't he? It's too bad he's married!"

"Maybe his wife doesn't think so."

"I mean, I'm a normal girl and I'm not old-fashioned, and the one thing I do miss here is a man to fight off. In fact, I'm beginning to feel that if one did come along I wouldn't even struggle."

"You sound as if that Scottish song was written about you," said the Saint, and he sang softly:

> *"Ilka lassie has her laddie,*
>   *Ne'er a ane ha' I;*
> *But all the lads they smile at me,*
>   *Comin' through the rye."*

She laughed.

"Well, at least you smiled at me, and that makes today look a little better."

"Where were you going?"

"To work. I just walked over across the fields—it's much shorter than by the lane."

Now that she mentioned it, he could see a glimpse of the Clanraith house between the trees. He turned and walked with her through the untidy little garden towards the Bastions' entrance.

"I'm sorry that stops me offering to take you on a picnic."

"I don't have any luck, do I? There's a dance in Fort Augustus tomorrow night, and I haven't been dancing for months, but I don't know a soul who'd take me."

"I'd like to do something about that," he said. "But it rather depends on what develops around here. Don't give up hope yet, though."

As they entered the hall, Bastion came out of a back room and said: "Ah, good morning, Annie. There are some pages I was revising last night on my desk. I'll be with you in a moment."

She went on into the room he had just come from, and he turned to the Saint.

"I suppose you didn't see anything."

"If we had, you'd've heard plenty of gunfire and hollering."

"Did you leave Eleanor down there?"

"Yes. But I don't think she's in any danger in broad daylight. Did Mackenzie call?"

"Not yet. I expect you're anxious to hear from him. The telephone's in the drawing-room—why don't you settle down there? You might like to browse through some of Eleanor's collection of books about the Monster."

Simon accepted the suggestion, and soon found himself so absorbed that only his empty stomach was conscious of the time when Bastion came in and told him that lunch was ready. Mrs. Bastion had already returned and was dishing up an agreeably aromatic lamb stew which she apologized for having only warmed up.

"You were right, it was just routine," she said. "A lot of waiting for nothing. But one of these days it won't be for nothing."

"I was thinking about it myself, dear," Bastion said, "and it seems to me that there's one bad weakness in your eight-hour-a-day system. There are enough odds against you already in only being able to see about a quarter of the loch, which leaves the Monster another three-quarters where it could just as easily pop up. But on top of that, watching only eight hours out of the twenty-four only gives us a one-third chance of being there even if it does pop up within range of our observation post. That doesn't add to the odds against us, it multiplies them."

"I know; but what can we do about it?"

"Since Mr. Templar pointed out that anyone should really be safe enough with a high-powered rifle in their hands and everyone else within call, I thought that three of us could divide up the watches and cover the whole day from before dawn till after dusk, as long as one could possibly see anything. That is, if Mr. Templar would help out. I know he can't stay here indefinitely, but——"

"If it'll make anybody feel better, I'd be glad to take a turn that way," Simon said indifferently.

It might have been more polite to sound more enthusiastic, but he could not make himself believe that the Monster would actually be caught by any such system. He was impatient for Mackenzie's report, which he thought was the essential detail.

The call came about two o'clock, and it was climactically negative.

"The doctor canna find a trrace o' drugs or poison in the puir animal."

Simon took a deep breath.

"What did he think of its injuries?"

"He said he'd ne'er seen the like o' them. He dinna ken anything in the wurruld wi' such crrushin' power in its jaws as yon monster must have. If 'twas no' for the teeth marrks, he wad ha' thocht it was done wi' a club. But the autopsy mak's that impossible."

"So I take it you figure that rules you officially out," said the Saint bluntly. "But give me a number where I can call you if the picture changes again."

He wrote it down on a pad beside the telephone before he turned and relayed the report.

"That settles it," said Mrs. Bastion. "It can't be anything else but *an Niseag*. And we've got all the more reason to try Noel's idea of keeping watch all day."

"I had a good sleep this morning, so I'll start right away," Bastion volunteered. "You're entitled to a siesta."

"I'll take over after that," she said. "I want to be out there again at twilight. I know I'm monopolizing the most promising times, but this matters more to me than to anyone else."

Simon helped her with the dishes after they had had coffee, and then she excused herself.

"I'll be fresher later if I do take a little nap. Why don't you do the same? It was awfully good of you to get up in the middle of the night with me."

"It sounds as if I won't be needed again until later tomorrow morning," said the Saint. "But I'll be reading and brooding. I'm almost as interested in *an Niseag* now as you are."

He went back to the book he had left in the drawing-room as the house settled into stillness. Annie Clanraith had already departed, before lunch, taking a sheaf of papers with her to type at home.

Presently he put the volume down on his thighs and lay passively thinking, stretched out on the couch. It was his uniquely personal method of tackling profound problems, to let himself relax into a state of blank receptiveness in which half-subconscious impressions could grow and flow together in delicately fluid adjustments that could presently mould a conclusion almost as concrete as knowledge. For some time he gazed sightlessly at the ceiling, and then he continued to meditate with his eyes closed . . .

He was awakened by Noel Bastion entering the room, humming tunelessly. The biographer of Wellington was instantly apologetic.

"I'm sorry, Templar—I thought you'd be in your room."

"That's all right." Simon glanced at his watch, and was

mildly surprised to discover how sleepy he must have been. "I was doing some thinking, and the strain must have been too much for me."

"Eleanor relieved me an hour ago. I hadn't seen anything, I'm afraid."

"I didn't hear you come in."

"I'm pretty quiet on my feet. Must be a habit I got from commando training. Eleanor often says that if she could stalk like me she'd have a lot more trophies." Bastion went to the bookcase, took down a book, and thumbed through it for some reference. "I've been trying to do some work, but it isn't easy to concentrate."

Simon stood up and stretched himself.

"I guess you'll have to get used to working under difficulties if you're going to be a part-time monster hunter for ten years—isn't that how long Eleanor said she was ready to spend at it?"

"I'm hoping it'll be a good deal less than that."

"I was reading in this book *More Than a Legend* that in 1934, when the excitement about the Monster was at its height, a chap named Sir Edward Mountain hired a bunch of men and organized a systematic watch like you were suggesting, but spacing them all around the lake. It went on for a month or two, and they got a few pictures of distant splashings, but nothing that was scientifically accepted."

Bastion put his volume back on the shelf.

"You're still sceptical, aren't you?"

"What I've been wondering," said the Saint, "is why this savage behemoth with the big sharp teeth and the nutcracker jaws chomped up a dog but didn't swallow even a little nibble of it."

"Perhaps it isn't carnivorous. An angry elephant will

mash a man to a pulp, but it won't eat him. And that dog could be very irritating, barking at everything——"

"According to what I heard, there wasn't any barking. And I'm sure the sheep it's supposed to have taken didn't bark. But the sheep disappeared entirely, didn't it?"

"That's what Clanraith says. But for all we know, the sheep may have been stolen."

"But that could have given somebody the idea of building up the Monster legend from there."

Bastion shook his head.

"But the dog *did* bark at everyone," he insisted stubbornly.

"Except the people he knew," said the Saint, no less persistently. "Every dog is vulnerable to a few people. You yourself, for instance, if you'd wanted to, could have come along, and if he felt lazy he'd've opened one eye and then shut it again and gone back to sleep. Now, are you absolutely sure that nobody else was on those terms with him? Could a postman or a milkman have made friends with him? Or anyone else at all?"

The other man massaged his moustache.

"I don't know . . . Well, perhaps Fergus Clanraith might."

Simon blinked.

"But it sounded to me as if he didn't exactly love the dog."

"Perhaps he didn't. But it must have known him pretty well. Eleanor likes to go hiking across country, and the dog always used to go with her. She's always crossing Clanraith's property and stopping to talk to him, she tells me. She gets on very well with him, which is more than I do."

"What, that old curmudgeon?"

"I know, he's full of that Scottish Nationalist nonsense.

But Eleanor is half Scots herself, and that makes her almost human in his estimation. I believe they talk for hours about salmon fishing and grouse shooting."

"I wondered if he had an appealing side hidden away somewhere," said the Saint thoughtfully, "or if Annie got it all from her mother."

Bastion's deep-set sooty eyes flickered over him appraisingly.

"She's rather an attractive filly, isn't she?"

"I have a feeling that to a certain type of man, in certain circumstances, and perhaps at a certain age, her appeal might be quite dangerous."

Noel Bastion had an odd expression of balancing some answer on the tip of his tongue, weighing it for advisability, changing his mind a couple of times about it, and finally swallowing it. He then tried to recover from the pause by making a business of consulting the clock on the mantelpiece.

"Will you excuse me? Eleanor asked me to bring her a thermos of tea about now. She hates to miss that, even for *an Niseag.*"

"Sure."

Simon followed him into the kitchen, where a kettle was already simmering on the black coal stove. He watched while his host carefully scalded a teapot and measured leaves into it from a canister.

"You know, Major," he said, "I'm not a detective by nature, even of the private variety."

"I know. In fact, I think you used to be just the opposite."

"That's true, too. I do get into situations, though, where I have to do a bit of deducing, and sometimes I startle everyone by coming up with a brilliant hunch. But as a general rule, I'd rather prevent a crime than solve one. As it says in your kind of textbooks, a little preventive action can save a lot of counter-attacks."

The Major had poured boiling water into the pot with a steady hand, and was opening a vacuum flask while he waited for the brew.

"You're a bit late to prevent this one, aren't you?—if it *was* a crime."

"Not necessarily. Not if the death of Golly was only a stepping-stone—something to build on the story of a missing sheep, and pave the way for the Monster's next victim to be a person. If a person were killed in a similar way now, the Monster explanation would get a lot more believers than if it had just happened out of the blue."

Bastion put sugar and milk into the flask, without measuring, with the unhesitating positiveness of practice, and took the lid off the teapot to sniff and stir it.

"But good heavens, Templar, who could treat a dog like that, except a sadistic maniac?"

Simon lighted a cigarette. He was very certain now, and the certainty made him very calm.

"A professional killer," he said. "There are quite a lot of them around who don't have police records. People whose temperament and habits have developed a great callousness about death. But they're not sadists. They're normally kind to animals and even to human beings, when it's normally useful to be. But fundamentally they see them as expendable, and when the time comes they can sacrifice them quite impersonally."

"I know Clanraith's a farmer, and he raises animals only to have them butchered," Bastion said slowly. "But it's hard to imagine him doing what you're talking about, much as I dislike him."

"Then you think we should discard him as a red herring?"

Bastion filled the thermos from the teapot, and capped it.

"I'm hanged if I know. I'd want to think some more about it. But first I've got to take this to Eleanor."

"I'll go with you," said the Saint.

He followed the other out of the back door. Outside, the dusk was deepening with a mistiness that was beginning to do more than the failing light to reduce visibility. From the garden, one could see into the orchard but not beyond it.

"It's equally hard for the ordinary man," Simon continued relentlessly, "to imagine anyone who's lived with another person as man and wife, making love and sharing the closest moments, suddenly turning around and killing the other one. But the prison cemeteries are full of 'em. And there are plenty more on the outside who didn't get caught—or who are still planning it. At least half the time, the marriage has been getting a bit dull, and someone more attractive has come along. And then, for some idiotic reason, often connected with money, murder begins to seem cleverer than divorce."

Bastion slackened his steps, half turning to peer at Simon from under heavily contracted brows.

"I'm not utterly dense, Templar, and I don't like what you seem to be hinting at."

"I don't expect you to, chum. But I'm trying to stop a murder. Let me make a confession. When you and Eleanor have been out or in bed at various times, I've done quite a lot of prying. Which may be a breach of hospitality, but it's less trouble than search warrants. You remember those scratches in the ground near the dead dog which I said could've been made with something that wasn't claws? Well, I found a gaff among somebody's fishing tackle that could've made them, and the point had fresh shiny scratches and even some mud smeared on it which can be analysed. I haven't been in the attic and found an embalmed shark's head with several teeth missing, but I'll bet Mackenzie could find one. And I haven't yet found the club with the teeth set in it, because I haven't yet been allowed down by the lake alone; but I think it's there somewhere, probably stuffed under a bush, and just waiting to be hauled out when the right head is turned the wrong way."

Major Bastion had come to a complete halt by that time.

"You unmitigated bounder," he said shakily. "Are you going to have the impertinence to suggest that I'm trying to murder my wife, to come into her money and run off with a farmer's daughter? Let me tell you that I'm the one who has the private income, and——"

"You poor feeble egotist," Simon retorted harshly, "I didn't suspect that for one second after she made herself rather acutely available to me, a guest in your house. She obviously wasn't stupid, and no girl who wasn't would have gambled a solid understanding with you against a transient flirtation. But didn't you ever read *Lady Chatterley's Lover*? Or the Kinsey Report? And hasn't it dawned on you that a forceful woman like Eleanor, just because she isn't a glamour girl, couldn't be bored to frenzy with a husband who only cares about the campaigns of Wellington?"

Noel Bastion opened his mouth, and his fists clenched, but whatever was intended to come from either never materialized. For at that moment came the scream.

Shrill with unearthly terror and agony, it split the darkening haze with an eldritch intensity that seemed to turn every hair on the Saint's nape into an individual icicle.

And it did not stop, but ululated again and again in weird cadences of hysteria.

For an immeasurable span they were both petrified; and then Bastion turned and began to run wildly across the meadow, towards the sound.

"*Eleanor*!" he yelled, insanely, in a voice almost as piercing as the screams.

He ran so frantically that the Saint had to call on all his reserves to make up for Bastion's split-second start. But he did close the gap as Bastion stumbled and almost fell over something that lay squarely across their path. Simon had seen it an instant sooner, and swerved, mechanically identifying the steely glint that had caught his eye as a reflection from a long gun-barrel.

And then, looking ahead and upwards, he saw through the blue fogginess something for which he would never completely believe his eyes, yet which would haunt him for the rest of his life. Something grey-black and scaly-slimy, an immense amorphous mass from which a reptilian neck and head with strange protuberances reared and swayed far up over him. And in the hideous dripping jaws something of human shape, from which the screams came, that writhed and flailed ineffectually with a peculiar-looking club . . .

With a sort of incoherent sob, Bastion scooped up the rifle at his feet and fired it. The horrendous mass convulsed; and into Simon's eardrums, still buzzing from the heavy blast, came a sickening crunch that cut off the last shriek in the middle of a note.

The towering neck corkscrewed with frightful power, and the thing that had been human was flung dreadfully towards them. It fell with a kind of soggy limpness almost at their feet, as whatever had spat it out lurched backwards and was blotted out by the vaporous dimness with the sound of a gigantic splash while Bastion was still firing again at the place where it had been . . .

As Bastion finally dropped the gun and sank slowly to his knees beside the body of his wife, Simon also looked down and saw that her hand was still spasmodically locked around the thinner end of the crude bludgeon in which had been set a row of shark's teeth. Now that he saw it better, he saw that it was no home-made affair, but probably a souvenir of some expedition to the South Pacific. But you couldn't be right all the time, about every last detail. Just as a few seconds ago, and until he saw Bastion with his head bowed like that over the woman who had plotted to murder him, he had never expected to be restrained in his comment by the irrational compassion that finally moved him.

"By God," he thought, "now I know I'm ageing."

But aloud he said: "She worked awful hard to sell everyone on the Monster. If you like, we can leave it that way. Luckily I'm a witness to what happened just now. But I don't have to say anything about—this."

He released the club gently from the grip of the dead fingers, and carried it away with him as he went to telephone Mackenzie.

THE LAST WORD

And so, my friends, dear bookworms, most noble fellow drinkers, frustrated burglars, affronted policemen, upright citizens with furled umbrellas and secret buccaneering dreams—that seems to be very nearly all for now. It has been nice having you with us, and we hope you will come again, not once, but many times.

Only because of our great love for you, we would like to take this parting opportunity of mentioning one small matter which we have very much at heart.

For that loyal and exclusive company who wanted a little closer contact with us than they could get by merely reading, Simon Templar and I founded, about fifteen years ago, THE SAINT CLUB. It is a pretty elastic organisation, and the rules are very much what you want to interpret them to be. The only one which we ruthlessly insist on is the annual minimum subscription of 5s. a year for readers over 16 years; 2s. 6d. a year for the under-16's. They are due on 1st August each year. We have to do this, because these funds assist the Arbour Youth Club in a blitzed East End area of London, a very charitable job in one of London's neediest and most neglected areas. If you would like to add your help, please write to the Hon. Secretary, THE SAINT CLUB, East Arbour Street, Stepney, London, E.1.

Which leaves me, I think, with only one more of those standard questions to forestall. You need not go on writing to ask me whether there are going to be more Saint Stories. The standing answer, now and as for as long as the pair of us can keep it up, is—

WATCH FOR THE SIGN OF THE SAINT

HE WILL BE BACK